HIDEOUT

DON'T MISS ANY ANTICS OF THE MAN WITH THE PLAN,
FROM GORDON KORMAN:

SWINDLE
ZOOBREAK
FRAMED
SHOWOFF

HIDEOUT

GORDON KORMAN

Scholastic Inc.

This book was originally published in hardcover by Scholastic Press in 2013.

ISBN 978-0-545-44867-3

12 11 10 9 8 7 6   16 17 18/0

Printed in the U.S.A.   40
First paperback printing, December 2013

The text was set in ITC Century.
Book design by Elizabeth B. Parisi and Whitney Lyle

For Michael and Trudy Iserson.
All hail the perfect couple,
50 years and going strong.

HIDEOUT

THE FIRST HIDEOUT

HISTORY'S MOST FAMOUS LOSERS:
CHRISTOPHER COLUMBUS: couldn't find Asia, largest continent on earth.
THE BUFFALO BILLS: made it to four straight Super Bowls, and lost them all.
K2: runner-up for world's highest mountain.
THE PRONGHORN ANTELOPE: not quite as fast as the cheetah.
LUTHOR:

G riffin Bing set down his pen. How could he begin to explain why Luthor, Savannah Drysdale's oversized Doberman, belonged on this list? Luthor had gotten himself disqualified from the Global Kennel Society Dog Show, minutes before he was about to win it all. Therefore, he was a loser. But he'd managed to lose so spectacularly that he was more famous by far than the poodle who'd actually won the top prize.

Ben Slovak, Griffin's best friend, stepped into Griffin's bedroom and asked, "Are you ready?"

"Almost," said Griffin. "I'm just finishing up the card."

Ben peered over his shoulder. "*That's* a birthday card? Calling Luthor a loser?"

"It's a compliment," Griffin insisted. "You just have to read between the lines."

"Savannah's going to feed you to the birthday boy!"

Griffin was stubborn. "Who has a birthday party for a dog, anyway?"

But neither friend had to answer that question. Everyone knew Savannah was the greatest animal lover and animal expert the town of Cedarville had ever known. In addition to Luthor, she was the house-mate—never say *owner*—of a capuchin monkey, two cats, four rabbits, seven hamsters, three turtles, a pack rat, a parakeet, and an albino chameleon.

"Let's go," Ben prodded. "Ferret Face has been looking forward to this all day. He can usually manage to snag a few bites of Luthor's dog food."

At the mention of his name, the little ferret poked his needle-like snout out of Ben's collar and looked around with black, beady eyes. He didn't live inside Ben's clothes; that was his workplace. Ben suffered from a condition called narcolepsy—he could fall asleep without warning at any time of the day or night. It was the ferret's job to administer a wake-up nip whenever he felt his master nodding off.

4

"Oh, all right," Griffin relented. On the card, he wrote:

Win or lose, Luthor's the best. Happy 5th, Big Guy.

By the time they got to the Drysdales', the party was in full swing. A picnic blanket had been spread in the living room, and Luthor sat at the head, all one hundred and fifty pounds of him, big black nose buried in a Bundt cake made of meat loaf. The human guests were giving him a fairly wide berth. Savannah's friends all remembered the guard dog that Luthor used to be. And although he was much calmer now, he always seemed ever-so-slightly unstable, as if a vicious beast might be lurking just below the surface.

The monkey Cleopatra, Luthor's closest friend, circulated among the partygoers with a tray of mini pizza bagels.

Griffin popped one into his mouth. "Thanks, Cleo," he said absently, like he was speaking to a waiter. In the Drysdale house, you almost never noticed the difference between people and animals. That's just the way it was.

Antonia Benson, who usually went by her rock-climbing nickname, Pitch, sidled up to him. "You missed *Pin the Tail on the Dogcatcher*. This party is the dumbest thing I've ever seen not on TV."

"Don't tell that to Savannah," Ben whispered nervously.

"It's going to get a lot better," Logan Kellerman assured them confidently. "As my present to Luthor, I'm going to perform the final scene in *Old Yeller*."

"You're kidding, right?" exclaimed Griffin. "You're going to be the kid who has to shoot his dog?"

"No," said Logan. "I'm going to be the dog."

"Kill me now," requested Pitch, "before I have to witness this."

Melissa Dukakis agitated her head, causing her curtain of hair to part and reveal her shy eyes. "How does Savannah even know when Luthor's real birthday is? She didn't get him as a puppy."

Savannah looked up from returning one of her rabbits to its cage. "It really is today. The tattoo inside his ear gave me the name of the breeder. It turns out Luthor was born in Germany. He was sold off because he was the runt of the litter, and that's how he came to America."

All the friends looked over at the former runt, whose mouth was open wide enough to accommodate a human head as he polished off the last of his meat loaf ring. Peering on from Ben's collar, Ferret Face heaved a sigh of disappointment.

"Anyway," Savannah continued, "there must have been a mix-up, because he was trained to be a guard dog." For a moment, her eyes filled with tears. "It's tragic. But it's all part of the sweet, wonderful, sensitive creature you see before you today."

An awkward silence followed, as everybody remembered being chased, cornered, barked at, and even snapped at by this sweet, wonderful, sensitive creature.

There was a cake for the people, too, with six candles—one for each of Luthor's five years, and one to grow on.

"Like *he* needs to grow!" Ben whispered.

They were in the middle of singing "Happy Birthday" when Luthor suddenly leaped up, overturning the cake plate and the table it stood on. The growl that came from his throat rattled the windows. The short hairs at the scruff of his neck stood straight up.

Ben crouched behind a chair. Inside his shirt, Ferret Face tried to burrow under one arm.

"Sweetie, what's the matter?" Savannah asked, alarmed.

The doorbell rang. The growl turned into a sharp bark.

Savannah threw open the door. There on the front step stood a short, stocky man in his thirties with curly hair exploding out from around an L.A. Dodgers baseball cap. He was smiling broadly, but his eyes, which appeared double-size behind Coke-bottle glasses, were not smiling at all.

"Savannah Drysdale! Lovely to see you again! Did you miss me?"

The shocked silence was punctuated only by Luthor's angry roaring. Cleopatra set down her tray and rushed to comfort her best friend.

Everyone knew the newcomer all too well. He was the last person anyone had expected to see — or wanted to.

S. Wendell Palomino, better known to Griffin and his friends as Swindle.

The name brought back horrible memories. Swindle had once owned the collectibles shop where Luthor had been a guard dog. The storekeeper had cheated Griffin out of a Babe Ruth baseball card worth nearly a million dollars. In the end, Swindle had left town in disgrace, deserting Luthor at the dog pound. Savannah had adopted him instantly. It had all worked out okay.

Or so everyone had thought.

"What's *he* doing here?" Pitch demanded, voicing the question on all their minds.

Swindle beamed. "Simple, little lady. I'm not here to trouble any of you young people. I just came to pick up my dog."

The collective gasp nearly sucked all the air out of the house.

Savannah found her voice at last. "*Your* dog? You abandoned him!"

Palomino's smile didn't waver. "We got separated a while back," he admitted. "I appreciate your looking out for him while I was tracking him down again."

"I don't *look out* for Luthor!" Savannah almost blew a gasket. "He's a part of me, and I'm a part of him, and we love each other with all our souls! Someone like you wouldn't know anything about that! I'm amazed you bothered to drop him at the pound instead of leaving him to starve! If it hadn't been for me—"

Swindle's smile turned suddenly ugly. "If it hadn't been for you kids, I would still have my business and my home and my good reputation in this community! All I have left is my beloved pet."

Griffin could always smell a rat, and the rat smell coming off of Swindle had nothing to do with Savannah's menagerie of pets. "Wait a minute!" he said. "You don't care about Luthor! You've been reading about how he almost won the big dog show! You just want him because you think he'll make you some money! That's low, even for you!"

Palomino's huge eyes narrowed. "Don't think I've forgotten *you*, sonny boy. Your little plan ruined my life! Lucky for you, I've got no hard feelings. I'll take my dog and be on my way."

Griffin stepped in front of the Doberman, his arms folded in front of him. "If you want Luthor, you're going to have to go through me."

"And me," Ben added immediately, joining his friend. Ferret Face appeared out of his collar, looking defiant.

One by one, the others formed a phalanx between the Doberman and his former owner.

Luthor let out an angry bark, as if letting them all know that he was quite capable of protecting himself.

Swindle reversed a step. "Funny thing. The dog pound can't find any paperwork from when I supposedly left Luthor there." He turned to address Savannah. "Which means you never legally adopted him, since he wasn't free to be legally adopted. At least, that's what my lawyer says."

That was all Savannah needed to hear. *"Mom! Dad!"*

Her parents were out of earshot in the backyard, laying down a portable doggie dance floor. Pitch ran to get them, but Swindle held his ground on the doorstep.

"The law's on my side," he said with sinister glee. "I will get my dog back. And when I do, I'll make sure you never, ever see him again."

With that, S. Wendell Palomino spun on his heel and left. By the time Mr. and Mrs. Drysdale came running in with Pitch, he was gone.

The party was over.

The Inn at Cedarville occupied a beautiful stone structure that had originally been built before the Civil War.

"He has to be a guest here," Griffin explained to Ben as they entered the lobby. "It's the only hotel in town."

"Right," Ben agreed nervously. "He can't be staying with friends. Who'd be friends with a creep like Swindle?"

Griffin picked up a house phone. "Swindle's—I mean, S. Wendell Palomino's room, please," he told the operator.

When the woman put the call through, Griffin flashed his friend a triumphant grin. But after several rings brought no reply, he hung up, deflated. "He's not there."

Ben's sigh was one part disappointment and ninety-nine parts relief. "Let's get out of here. My mother told me not to go anywhere near Swindle now that he's back in town."

Griffin's sharp eyes scanned the lobby, lighting on a pudgy figure alone at a table in the restaurant. "There he is. He's having breakfast."

The boys entered the small coffee shop and approached their enemy. "Sorry to disturb you, Mr. Palomino," Griffin said.

Swindle fixed them with a phony smile. "Well, what have we here? A delegation from the Breaking and Entering Club. I thought you might show up."

"We just wanted to say we're sorry we caused you so much trouble last time," Griffin lied. In reality, he wasn't sorry at all. On the contrary, he had never been quite so thrilled with the way one of his plans had worked out. "We didn't mean to close down your store and get you run out of town."

Palomino leaned back from his breakfast. "Well, sonny boy, sorry doesn't butter the biscuit. So you can tell your friend Savannah that I'm still taking back my dog, no matter how sorry everybody is."

Griffin hung his head. "We're okay with that. Even Savannah understands. We won the last round, and you won this one."

"We've got no hard feelings," Ben added, holding Ferret Face inside his shirt to prevent him from making a dive for Swindle's side order of sausage.

Palomino beamed all over his nasty face. "Really? No kidding."

Griffin nodded. "But just between us, you *did* give

up that dog, didn't you? It's just bad luck that the Cedarville pound lost the proof."

Swindle yawned elaborately, stretching his arms over his head. Then, in a lightning move, he reached across the table and ripped open the front of Griffin's shirt, sending buttons flying. There, taped to the chest of The Man With The Plan, was a small recorder, operating light flashing.

"What am I supposed to say, that I lied about not giving up the dog? Fine — I'm wrong; you're right. And good luck playing this for anybody." He ripped the small machine off Griffin's skin, and plopped it into his orange juice. "Oops."

Griffin stared in dismay. He'd only bought the recorder yesterday for this particular mission. "Aw, come on, Mr. Palomino! Can't we let bygones be bygones?"

"They're not bygones to me!" Swindle snapped. "You kids wrecked my life and there's payback for that! I'm taking the dog. He's worth a fortune on the show circuit, and with the breeders after that. And when he's no good for that anymore, I'll sell him to the highest bidder, and I don't care if he ends up guarding a junkyard in Death Valley, where the rattlesnakes will show him who's boss."

Ben was so horrified that he let go of Ferret Face, who devoured half a sausage patty before he could be recaptured. "You can't mean that!"

"I'm not finished," Palomino said with diabolical satisfaction. "Once I've squeezed every cent I can get out of that mangy mutt, I'm coming back to Cedarville, where I'm going to make a career out of *you*."

"Us?" the boys chorused.

"I intend to devote my time and considerable fortune to making your lives miserable."

Griffin reddened. "You can't get away with harassing people who haven't done anything wrong."

Swindle fished the dripping recorder out of his juice. "Neither of you lunkheads has the brains to rig something like this, so I'm guessing this is the work of your electronically gifted friend Melissa. Well, the next time she hacks into some secure website where she's not supposed to be, I'll be there to tell the police exactly who to talk to. When there are footprints on someone's roof, I'll point out the Benson girl. Hacker, climber, actor, animal trainer. And you and your little flunky—one step out of line and you're done. I'll have you all up on charges, and I won't back down until I've blackened your lives the way you blackened mine. Thinking of going to college, getting a decent job? Not with your records. You'll rue the day you ever heard the name S. Wendell Palomino. Now get out. You've already ruined my orange juice!"

Griffin and Ben were too shocked to reply. It had been Griffin's idea to try to trick a recorded confession out of Swindle, but the ploy had more than backfired. Neither could have imagined the terrible anger of this man, who technically had nothing to be angry about. *He* was the thief who had cheated *them*. They had merely taken back what was rightfully theirs.

At that moment, Palomino's intentions became clear in all their elaborate malice. No planner could fail to recognize someone else's plan. Luthor was only the beginning. This went far beyond money or a show dog.

It was Swindle's revenge.

EXCERPT FROM COURT TRANSCRIPT 5037221,
STATE OF NEW YORK, COUNTY OF NASSAU
THE HONORABLE JUDGE FRANKLIN BITTNER
PRESIDING . . .

. . . Since there is no evidence that Mr. Palomino ever relinquished ownership of the dog, Luthor, it is the decision of this court that Ms. Drysdale's adoption was never legal and binding. Therefore, the court finds in favor of the plaintiff, S. Wendell Palomino, and further orders Ms. Drysdale to turn Luthor over to his rightful owner on or before August 9, 12 p.m., Eastern Daylight Saving Time . . .

Griffin and Ben had expected floods of tears from poor Savannah when the court's decision came down. But her cold fury was infinitely more terrible to behold. She paced around Griffin's room like a caged tiger, her normally fair features red and approaching magenta.

"What kind of stupid judge makes a decision like that without even asking Luthor what he prefers? How can he give that sweet, innocent, sensitive animal to *Swindle*, of all people? Anyone who bothers to look can see that Luthor hates him!"

"Maybe that's the answer right there," Ben put in. "We don't have to do anything to stop Swindle. Luthor's all the firepower we need. The first minute Swindle turns his back, Luthor'll have his lungs out and be hanging them off the chandelier!"

"That's even worse!" Savannah exclaimed in horror. "Do you know what happens to a dog who attacks a human? He gets put down because he's vicious! Luthor's not vicious; he wouldn't hurt a fly!"

"Face it, Savannah," said Ben quietly. "He would hurt a fly. I mean, I like him, too. But he would hurt a whole swarm of flies."

Griffin was finding Savannah's anger contagious. "Swindle!" he spat. "I never thought that guy would have the nerve to show his face in Cedarville again! You think he cares whether Luthor likes him or not? Forget it! To him, a famous dog is no different than a Babe Ruth card—money in the bank!"

"Can't your parents appeal the judge's decision?" Ben asked Savannah. "On TV, that kind of case stretches on for years."

"We thought of that, too," she replied miserably. "Our lawyer says we'd still have to give up Luthor while the appeal is pending. I can't hand him over to that awful man, not even for five minutes!"

Griffin shook his head. "That's no good. By the time the appeal goes through, Swindle will already be rich off Luthor, and heading back east to use his money to ruin our lives."

Savannah was disgusted. "Luthor's in danger, but let's never forget that this is really all about *you*."

"It's about every single one of us!" Ben insisted. "He's out to get you, too. He said so! I heard it with my own ears."

"I don't care about myself; I care about Luthor! We need a *plan*!"

"Swindle has a court order," Griffin tried to explain. "If you don't obey it, you're breaking the law."

She was adamant. "We've broken the law before when we knew we were doing the right thing. This is the right thing. Nothing's ever been this right!"

"It's more like we *bent* the law," Griffin amended. "But you can't bend giving Swindle the dog. You either do it or you don't."

"Maybe it won't be so bad," Ben offered unhappily. "We're all going off to camp next week, so you won't be here for the actual — you know — thing. And by the time you get back, it'll all be done."

Her glance scorched Ben and caused Ferret Face to take cover inside his shirt. "You're out of your mind if you think I could go to camp with this hanging over Luthor's head! I'd sooner take him and run away from home!"

A thoughtful expression spread across Griffin's face. Savannah was too emotionally upset to notice it, but Ben knew exactly what it signified. It was a plan being born.

"Maybe," Griffin said in an odd voice, "you can do both."

Savannah looked impatient. "What are you talking about? Do both what?"

"Go to camp *and* keep Luthor out of Swindle's clutches."

Ben was beginning to clue in. "Are you thinking what I think you're thinking? No way would that ever work!"

"Any plan can work," Griffin lectured, "if you take the time to plot out the details and prepare for every possibility."

"Would you guys mind telling me what you're talking about?" Savannah interrupted in agitation.

The Man With The Plan smiled. "Welcome to Operation Hideout."

Mrs. Drysdale stuffed a pair of flip-flops into the zipper pocket of Savannah's duffel. "Okay — that's five shorts, three bathing suits, and fourteen T-shirts. I've sewn your name into everything until my fingers are nothing but stumps!"

"Thanks, Mom." Savannah placed a hoodie on top of the pile. "It might get cooler at night."

Mrs. Drysdale smiled. "I can't tell you how proud I am about the way you're handling all this. I know how much Luthor means to you."

Savannah offered a melancholy shrug. "Maybe we'll win the appeal," she said without much conviction. "I just wish Luthor didn't have to go with that awful jerk until it gets decided."

Her mother sighed. "Well, I'm just glad you're not going to let it ruin camp for you. Dad and I were afraid you'd refuse to go."

"What would I do here, besides sit around and be miserable? All my friends will be at some camp or other. Besides, it isn't going to help poor Luthor if I drive myself crazy worrying about how Swindle's treating him."

"Very sensible attitude," Mrs. Drysdale approved. "By the way, where *is* Luthor? I haven't seen him all morning."

"Oh, you know — around."

Her mother paused, frowning. "A hundred-and-fifty-pound Doberman is not something you overlook. Aside from all that barking, he's a physical presence, knocking things over, and bumping into furniture."

They searched the house. Luthor was nowhere to be found.

"Oh, no!" Savannah cried. "Swindle's kidnapped him!"

"Why would he do that?" Mrs. Drysdale demanded.

"He has a court order on his side. He'll get the dog in a few days anyway."

"Then Luthor must have run away," Savannah decided. "Who can blame him? Would you want to go live with a mean, sleazy con man instead of the people who love you?"

Her mother regarded her intently. "Luthor's bright, but no dog could understand how court orders and appeals work."

"Luthor may not understand the legal system," said Savannah stubbornly, "but he's a beautiful, sensitive creature with amazing intuition. He feels how upset we are, and he can read the nasty, self-satisfied smirk on Swindle. He knows he's in trouble, and that money-grubbing animal abuser is at the heart of it. That must be why he ran away."

Her mother stared at her long and hard. "Well, in that case, we'd better find him. If the ninth comes along and we don't have a dog to turn over, the judge is going to want to know why."

"It isn't *our* fault Luthor ran away," Savannah reasoned weakly.

"Let's hope not." Her mother peered at her suspiciously. "By the way, when was the last time you talked to Griffin Bing?"

4

L uthor peered into the basement through the open casement window. It didn't look like a place where he wanted to go. He wheeled his big head around and growled at Griffin and Ben.

"I don't like the sound of that," said Ben nervously. "Now that he's out of the dog show, he's turning back into the old Luthor, and that's bad news."

"We need you inside," Griffin explained to the Doberman. "It's only temporary. You're going somewhere different after that."

Luthor didn't budge.

Griffin was becoming annoyed. "You always seem to understand when *Savannah*'s doing the talking."

"You're not a trained dog whisperer," his best friend noted.

Logan, Pitch, and Melissa appeared below them in the basement.

"All I could find was a piece of salami," Logan told them, holding the snack up. "Will that work?"

With a bark that was more like a roar, Luthor went for the meat, falling through the window into the darkened basement. Griffin and Ben quickly climbed in after him, lowering themselves to the floor.

"Why does it have to be *my* basement?" Logan complained. "It's not *my* dog."

"We'll all be on the firing line if Swindle gets his way," Griffin reminded him.

Logan was not sold. "It's *your* plan, Griffin. Why can't we use your place?"

Griffin shook his head. "No good. If the Drysdales get suspicious, my house will be the first place they look. Besides, you've had so much water damage that your mom refuses to come down here because the place is full of spiders. It's safe."

"What if one of the 'spiders' starts to bark?" Logan persisted.

Griffin put a hand on his friend's shoulder. "Look at it as an acting job. You're playing a character who *doesn't* have a Doberman in his basement."

"Got it." The idea intrigued Logan, and he tested out a few possible lines of dialogue:

"Pardon me, Mom? No, I didn't hear anything. . . . Barking? That was distant thunder. Or maybe one of those new European motor scooters. Their engines are very doglike . . . *To bay or not to bay? That is the question—*"

"Don't get fancy," Pitch advised. "If you try to be Shakespeare, you'll mess it up for sure."

"It's only for a couple of days," Griffin added. "Once we head into the woods for camp, Luthor disappears. This is a temporary safe house until we smuggle him onto the bus."

That was the backbone of Operation Hideout. It was designed to keep Luthor out of Swindle's greedy clutches while the Drysdales pursued their court appeal.

Melissa's beady eyes gazed out from behind her curtain of hair. "How is Savannah going to hide him for an entire month of camp? He's kind of tough to miss."

"It's not going to be easy," Griffin admitted. "But I'm going to Ebony Lake, too. I'll be right across the compound in the boys' cabins. When I get a look at the camp, I'll have to do some planning on the fly."

As Griffin and Ben walked home from the Kellerman house, Ben announced, "You know, Griffin, I was kind of bummed when I found out that I couldn't go to the same camp as you because Ebony Lake won't take Ferret Face. But I have to admit I'm not sorry to miss out on four weeks of Operation Hideout. Luthor's a suburban dog. Who knows what he's going to be like when you get him in the middle of nowhere. He could join a wolf pack or something."

"Don't be so dramatic," Griffin scoffed. "You're forgetting Savannah's going to be there. She can handle him."

Ben nodded. "Except when she's swimming. Or hiking. Or asleep. A time bomb doesn't always go off when it's convenient, you know. It goes off when it goes off."

Griffin was disgusted. "How many plans have we done together? And how many times has something gone wrong?"

"About fifty," Ben said feelingly. "And something goes wrong every single time. Usually more than once."

"But in the end it always works out okay," Griffin added.

Ben's mother was on the front porch of the Slovak house. She waved urgently as the boys approached. "Benjamin, Savannah's parents were just here. They tell me Luthor's gone missing. Do you and Griffin know anything about that?"

Ben froze, but Griffin was ready with a reply. "No, Mrs. Slovak, we don't know anything about Luthor being missing."

"That's a relief." She sighed, and went back inside.

Ben wheeled on his friend. "Way to go, Griffin. Now when this blows up in our faces, we're going to be in twice as much trouble for lying!"

"We didn't lie," Griffin said reasonably. "Luthor isn't missing. We know exactly where he is. Relax, Ben. Personally, I'm not worried about this plan at all."

Ben bit his tongue and said nothing. When Griffin wasn't worried, it was usually time to start worrying.

5

The front hall was clogged with the biggest piece of luggage anyone had ever seen. It looked like a regular hockey equipment bag, only longer, and on wheels. The tag read: *Griffin Bing, Camp Ebony Lake.*

When Mr. Drysdale pulled up into the Bings' driveway to pick up Griffin and deliver him to the camp bus, all he could do was stare.

"What have you got in there? Camp lasts four weeks, not four years!"

Griffin grinned. "Oh, you know—just some of my stuff."

"I packed a lot of things, too," Savannah put in nervously, trying to distract attention from her friend's enormous duffel.

It didn't work. "You're supposed to be leaving home, not taking it with you!" her father exclaimed in amazement.

It took both fathers and both campers to wrestle it into the back of the SUV.

Mr. Bing arched his back, groaning. "A few of the necessities of life, huh, Griffin?"

Griffin laughed uncomfortably, hugged his parents good-bye, and got into the SUV. It was only a two-minute ride, but Mr. Drysdale could not keep his eyes off the rearview mirror and the giant duffel that obscured the back window.

Finally, he stomped too hard on the brakes, and pulled over to the side. "Sorry, Griffin, but I'm going to have to see what's in that bag."

Savannah nearly jumped out of her skin. "There's no time, Dad! We'll miss our bus!"

"It'll only take a second," he assured her. "I'm just going to check inside."

Griffin shrugged. "Sure. Why not?"

The look Savannah shot him was nothing short of a horror mask.

Mr. Drysdale popped the rear access and unzipped the giant bag.

Savannah closed her eyes and waited for the world to end.

"Books?" her father questioned.

"Oh, Dad. You can't just let—" She stopped herself just in time. "Books?"

The inside of the duffel was stuffed with enough paperbacks to start a lending library.

"I never pegged you as such a reader," Mr. Drysdale told Griffin. "You've got more books than clothes in here." He shook his head. "I could have sworn—

never mind. Sorry I brought it up."

"That's okay," said Griffin graciously.

The bus to Camp Ebony Lake was parked on Seventh Street, beside a grove of tall trees. Mr. Drysdale loaded Savannah's bag in the luggage bay, then, with great difficulty, shoved Griffin's in beside it.

"Okay, you guys, have a great time. Uh — happy reading, Griffin. Try to get out some." He kissed his daughter, shook hands with her friend, and drove off.

As soon as he was gone, Savannah wheeled on Griffin. "What's going on?" she hissed. "Where's Luthor?"

Griffin was already hauling the enormous duffel out of the bus. "I had a panic attack last night that someone would unzip the bag, and there he'd be." He dragged the luggage on its wheels into the stand of maples, opened it, and began tossing books in all directions. Then he let out a high-pitched whistle.

Luthor was on them in an instant, hauling Logan and Ben at the end of his leash. The big Doberman jumped all over Savannah, deliriously happy to see her after his imprisonment in Logan's basement. Savannah was nearly as wild, planting kisses all over his huge head and snout, murmuring, "It's okay, sweetie. Everything's going to be fine."

"He wrecked our basement, you know," Logan said bitterly. "And my folks think *I* did it. You should see how it feels when your own parents believe you chewed up a beanbag chair! After camp, I have to go into therapy."

"Let's hurry up and get Luthor in the bag," Ben urged, Ferret Face peering out of his sleeve. "If you miss the bus, all this is for nothing."

It took Savannah's renowned skill as a dog whisperer to coax Luthor into the giant duffel. But he went, and lay down obediently, and even shut his eyes when she told him it was time to sleep. He objected a little when Griffin closed the zipper over his head, but Savannah's constant soothing voice managed to calm him.

"Well, have a good time—I guess," Ben said dubiously. "I'll text when I get to my camp."

The friends said good-bye, and Griffin and Savannah dragged the duffel, now even heavier than before, toward their bus.

"Whoa! No way!" the driver exclaimed. "You're not taking that on board. Load it into the baggage compartment."

"I can't," Griffin explained. "It has my computer in it. I promised my mom I wouldn't let it out of my sight."

"Fine. Take the computer out and stow that bag. We've got to get rolling. I swear—you kids bring more stuff every year! What have you got in there—a pool table?"

In resignation, Griffin and Savannah dragged their precious cargo around the side of the bus. Savannah opened the zipper a few inches, and leaned close.

"You're not going to like it, sweetie, but you have to be patient and stay calm." From her backpack she produced a handful of dog biscuits and a plastic baby bottle filled with water. "Be a good boy, okay?" She kissed his nose and zipped him in again, leaving enough room for some air to get in.

They re-boarded and settled in for the three-hour ride. The driver shut the door and put the engine in gear. The bus was actually beginning to pull out into traffic when there was a pounding on the door, and a foghorn voice called, "Wait! There's one more!"

The driver opened up and a large, stocky boy panted aboard, dragging a brass-bound trunk.

"Thanks, mister!" His piggy eyes met Griffin's horrified ones. "Hey, Bing! You're going to this camp, too?"

Darren Vader was the last person you wanted around when there was a plan in progress. He was a cheater and a snitch, and nothing gave him greater pleasure than to get Griffin into trouble.

"Listen, Darren," Griffin said reasonably. "Camp is supposed to be fun, so let's make a deal: I don't know you, and you don't know me, and we stay out of each other's way."

The big boy flopped down in the seat in front of Griffin. "Not gonna happen," he chortled with cruel satisfaction.

The howling began five minutes over the Whitestone Bridge.

"Man, does this bus ever need a tune-up!" complained the driver.

6

Camp Ebony Lake was a breathtaking spot in the deep woods of New York's Catskill Mountains, a circle of log cabins and small buildings surrounded by playing fields reclaimed from the dense forest. The lake itself was a vast black mirror, usually dead calm. According to the scientists at the research installation on the opposite shore, it was deeper in some places than Scotland's famous Loch Ness.

The tires crunched the gravel of the roadway as the bus pulled up to the main building. "Last stop, you guys," the driver announced. "Just give me a minute to pop open the cargo bay, and you can get your gear." He jumped to the ground, walked around the side of the bus, released the catch, and rolled up the panel to the baggage compartment.

He never saw it coming. With a terrifying roar, a large animal exploded out of the hold, flattening him to the turf. Dazed, he was aware of a huge black-and-brown body passing over him. Then the beast was gone, disappearing into the woods. There was the crackle of breaking branches as the monster fled, followed by silence. Whatever had been there was gone.

Alarmed, the campers poured off the bus, coming to the aid of their fallen driver.

"What happened?" asked one girl.

The driver sat up, catching his breath. "I — I opened the door, and a bear attacked me and ran into the forest!"

Griffin and Savannah exchanged an agonized look. Griffin's eyes traveled into the compartment. His huge bag looked suspiciously flat, with a great ragged hole chewed into the side. He put out a hand to stop Savannah from running off into the woods.

"Later!" he hissed.

"But—"

"Later!"

"We closed that hatch in Long Island," Darren Vader reasoned. "It couldn't have been a bear. Maybe a raccoon."

"I know what a raccoon looks like, kid," the driver retorted. "This was bigger."

"What about a cougar?" suggested someone else.

"Or a deer."

"Or a giant squirrel."

"There's no such thing!"

Eventually, Cyrus, the head counselor, took charge of the situation. "Guys, I've been here for twelve years, and there are no bears, no cougars, and no giant squirrels. Frogs, birds, and mosquitoes are more our speed. And whatever it was, it's gone now. So get your bunk assignments off the list and stow your gear."

Savannah sidled up to Griffin. "We have to find Luthor before he gets lost!"

"If we go now, we'll get caught," Griffin reasoned. "Even if nobody sees us, our counselors will know that we never showed up in our cabins. The last thing we need is to attract attention, especially with Vader in camp. Later, when everybody's asleep, we'll go after Luthor. He'll come running when he hears your voice."

"How can you be sure of that? A domestic animal won't do well in the wild!"

Griffin was exasperated. "Do you honestly think there's anything out there scarier than Luthor? You may be the animal expert, but I'm the planner. You've got to trust me. If we let on that Luthor's up here, we might as well just hand him to Swindle on a silver platter."

It was that final argument that won her over. Somehow she would have to get through this day for Luthor's sake.

Griffin was in Cabin 14 with Darren Vader. In fact, they were bunkmates, with Griffin on the bottom.

"Hey, Bing, I hope you're a sound sleeper, because I snore."

Griffin had discovered long ago that there no way to deal with Darren. If you fought back, it only encouraged him. And if you ignored him, he just pumped up the volume. Resignedly, he began to unpack, finding in dismay that Luthor had chewed through his clothes in order to get to the side of the bag. Shorts, T-shirts, and bathing suits were all cut to ribbons and damp with drool. He had packed enough for a month, but now he had clothes to last for three days at the most.

Marty, the Cabin 14 counselor, sat down beside Griffin as he was holding up a pair of underwear that looked like it had been through an atomic blast. Quickly, Griffin tried to hide the evidence.

But Marty smiled. "Don't be embarrassed. I understand that money's tight for families these days."

Griffin stared at him. *He thinks I packed clothes like shredded cobwebs because this is the best I've got?* The tricky part was that the guy could never be told the truth without revealing the whole story of Luthor in the luggage.

"There's a fund for campers in your situation," Marty told him. "We'll get you some better stuff. Don't worry."

"Thanks," he said, and almost strangled on the word.

The day dragged. Griffin had been looking forward to camp. But every swing of a bat and kick of a ball, every swimming stroke or bite of food in the mess hall seemed like a colossal waste of important time.

For him, there was no agony quite like a plan unfinished, with details left up in the air. Every time he caught sight of Savannah with the girls' group, he could tell she was thinking the exact same thing. And, like his, her eyes were following the sun in its path across the sky, waiting for the moment when they could spring into action and go after Luthor.

After dinner, there was a huge bonfire on the beach. And as they roasted marshmallows and sang songs, the counselors began to tell ghost stories, which were supposed to be scary, but really weren't.

"Boring!" called a voice that Griffin recognized as Darren's.

"Tell the real story!" piped up someone else. And a few of the older kids took up the cry.

"No way," said Cyrus seriously. "These new campers aren't ready for — that kind of information."

Well, that did it. A howl went up, demanding the truth, the whole truth, and nothing but the truth.

"All right," Cyrus said finally. "But don't come crying to me if you have nightmares about — the mechanical monster of Ebony Lake."

A shiver ran through the throng, but they hung in there, waiting for the story.

"You've all heard of the Loch Ness Monster. Well, Ebony Lake had a monster of its own — some sort of giant prehistoric fish that never evolved into a modern species because it lived in the inky depths of our lake, unchanged since the time of the dinosaurs."

The head counselor went on to explain that, forty years ago, a famous scientist by the name of Randolph Zim became a hermit and built himself a cabin on the lake, perhaps three quarters of a mile from the spot where they now sat. Zim was crazy, but he was also a renowned genius who used his skills to communicate with the monster.

"A terrible winter came along," Cyrus continued, "and the cabin was snowed in for months. The food ran out, and Zim knew that he would soon starve. There was only one source of food—the monster. So Zim took a sharp knife and cut off a fin, just enough to keep himself alive. But he felt sorry for his friend's pain, so he created a mechanical fin to replace the one he had eaten. As the winter went on and the deep freeze continued, Zim was forced to eat more and more of his only friend—until nothing remained except a great machine, a gleaming animatronic replica of the original monster. Now completely out of food, Zim starved to death. His frozen corpse was found in the cabin that spring.

"But the machine lives on. No one knows what it's thinking, or even if it thinks at all. Does it seek revenge for what a human did to it? Because it's now a machine, can it ever die? Are people in danger from it? We can't say. But every now and then, one of our campers sees it breaking the surface—the mechanical monster of Ebony Lake."

The silence that greeted the end of this grisly tale

was nearly total. Haunted eyes panned the black water, as if expecting the monster to menace the camp at any moment.

"Well," said Cyrus, "you wanted to know."

Out of this entire story, The Man With The Plan had taken only a single detail: There was an old cabin three-quarters of a mile down the shore.

What an excellent place to hide a dog on the lam.

Savannah lay in her upper bunk, her eyes closed, trying to keep track of the steady breathing around her. Only when all seven cabinmates were comfortably asleep would she be able to sneak out and meet Griffin.

Hurry up! she exhorted the lone holdout, probably that skinny girl from Boston. *Count sheep!* No doubt the poor kid was still shaking from that hideous story they'd all just heard. Under the covers, she clutched her flashlight a little tighter. She probably would have been scared herself if there weren't something ten thousand times more important going on.

Oh, please, let Luthor be okay. Griffin may have been The Man With The Plan, but he didn't know much about animals. What if that sweet puppy had gotten it into his beautiful mind to try to navigate his way back to Cedarville? They'd never find him then. And even if he made it, he'd be delivering himself right into the clutches of S. Wendell Palomino!

At last, the deep, even breathing from seven girls

told her that the coast was clear. She kicked into her sneakers and stole out of the cabin. Her feet barely touching the ground, she scampered through the shadows to the meeting place—a small stand of bushes near the flagpole.

"Griffin!" she hissed.

No reply.

Oh, no! What if he fell asleep by mistake? Would she have the courage to wander around these woods alone? Of course she would! For Luthor, she would walk through fire!

But her planned heroics were not necessary. In another few seconds, Griffin was crouched there beside her.

"Sorry I'm late," he whispered. "Vader put a frog in my bed, and there was a big stink about it. It took forever to get people to sleep."

"Let's go," she urged. "I'm freaking out!"

The woods were so dense and so dark that their flashlight beams lit only a few feet in front of them. They didn't dare shout for fear of being heard back at camp. So they called softly:

"Luthor—"

"I'm here, sweetie . . . where are you?"

They walked into the woods as deep as they dared. There was no sign of the Doberman.

Griffin was becoming confused. "I thought dogs could smell their owners from miles away. You didn't take a shower, did you?"

"Luthor's not used to the wild," Savannah explained, her heart sinking. "There must be hundreds of unfamiliar scents out here distracting him. But maybe . . . Griffin, have you got your phone? Call my cell, right now!"

"Why? I'm standing right next to you."

"Just do it!"

Griffin hit her number on his speed dial.

Savannah set her volume up to maximum. Her ring tone seemed to reverberate all through the woods around them—Elvis Presley's "Hound Dog." It played for about fifteen seconds before going to voicemail. "Call again!"

Griffin did. "Hound Dog" rang through the forest. After eight tries, Savannah put down her phone, and the regular nighttime sounds of the woods returned.

Griffin sighed. "It was a good try, Savannah—"

And then a new noise joined the chirping of crickets and the calls of night birds, distant at first, but growing louder and closer by the second. Something was out there, and it was really moving! The faint snapping of twigs became a crashing through underbrush.

Savannah could not remain silent. "Luthor—sweetie!" The answering bark was almost human in its yearning.

The Doberman burst out of the trees straight into Savannah's arms, whimpering his love and relief.

Savannah whimpered back, "Luthor, I'm so sorry we have to do this to you! It's the only way to keep you safe!"

The reunion could have gone on all night, but Griffin stepped in to keep the plan moving along. They backtracked to the camp, skirting the bunks, cutting straight to the beach, and then east along the shore.

"Cyrus said the cabin was three-quarters of a mile away," Griffin mused, "but keep your eyes peeled. He's a counselor, not a mapmaker."

The going was tougher when the beach ended and they had to make their way over marshy terrain. Griffin's sneakers sank into the mud, adding yet another article of clothing that was beyond repair. He wondered if the "special fund" would cover a new pair of shoes.

They had been walking for about half an hour when they spotted an ancient rowboat, partially buried in the mud and silt of the shore.

"Where there's a boat . . ." Griffin began.

Savannah finished his thought: ". . . there's a person who owned it and sailed it. And that person had to live somewhere."

If it hadn't been for the full moon, they might very well have missed the cabin. It was ramshackle and overgrown by shrubs and tall grass. The roof sagged.

"Boy," Griffin breathed. "When I imagine a dead man's shack, this is pretty much it."

Savannah was determined to show Luthor that all was well. She believed that even though animals couldn't always understand your words, your tone of voice communicated a much more important message. "Isn't this wonderful, sweetie? And you have it all to yourself." They stepped inside, scattering a family of field mice. "And lots of new friends for company."

"The only thing missing is the frozen body of Randolph Zim," Griffin added. "Or maybe that's buried under the floorboards."

"It's a wonderful place," Savannah said firmly, "and Luthor loves it."

The Doberman certainly didn't mind eating in his new home. Savanna popped open the can of dog food she had brought, and Luthor fell on the offering like a starving shark.

Griffin had a practical question. "What if he takes off again? He chewed through a zippered bag—not to mention all my clothes. This rickety old dump won't hold him. There's no glass in the windows, and the door won't even latch."

Savannah nodded reluctantly. "We'll have to tie him. But I want him to have a long lead. If he feels like a prisoner, he'll fight to get away." She got down on her knees and attached the leash to the handle of a heavy iron water pump.

Griffin looked grim. "It's nothing compared with the kind of prisoner he'll be if Swindle gets hold of him."

Judge Franklin Bittner leaned over his desk and peered down at Mr. and Mrs. Drysdale. "What do you mean 'disappeared'?"

"I know it sounds suspicious, considering the circumstances," Mr. Drysdale tried to explain. "But we think he ran away. It's been three days, and no one's seen hide nor hair of him. We've contacted animal control, and there are no Dobermans anywhere in the county."

"Why don't you try contacting your own kid?" S. Wendell Palomino accused angrily. "Or one of her accomplices, like that Bing delinquent?"

"Savannah is at camp right now," Mrs. Drysdale defended her daughter. "And so are all her friends. None of them had anything to do with Luthor running away."

Swindle spread his arms wide. "Your Honor—really? Doesn't this all seem convenient? The kids disappear and Luthor does, too? Don't you see this is just a scam to keep my dog from me?"

"I'll be the judge of that," Bittner said mildly. "That's why they call me 'judge.'"

"But, Your Honor, you're a reasonable man!" Palomino pleaded. "This is so obvious! Coincidences like this don't happen in real life!"

"You'd be surprised at the coincidences you see when you sit on this bench, Mr. Palomino. But—" He turned steely gray eyes to the Drysdales. "If it turns out that this is *not* a coincidence, you'll learn that violating a court order has very serious consequences."

8

From: Ben
To: Griffin
How is the "package"?

From: Griffin
To: Ben
Package safe. Ate my clothes, though. How's camp?

From: Ben
To: Griffin
Lame. The food gives Ferret Face gas. Pitch is here, too, star camper. Any news about Swindle?

From: Griffin
To: Ben
Made big trouble for Savannah's parents on handover day. All talk, no action, so far.

Orienteering was one of the top activities at Camp Ebony Lake since the dense trees provided such a challenge to anyone navigating with a compass. It was also one of the few activities where boys and girls competed together. So Griffin and Savannah made sure they were partners for the next day's competition.

"This is perfect," Griffin murmured as they marched through the underbrush, consulting their instruction sheet not at all. "Getting lost is part of the sport. So no one's going to ask any questions when we disappear."

"So long as we get to see Luthor," Savannah said fervently. "I can't bear the thought of him out there, all alone."

Griffin tried to perk up her spirits. "He can take care of himself. It's not like the mechanical monster's going to come out of the lake and eat him."

Savannah glared at him. "If that's your idea of humor—"

"Oh, please," Griffin scoffed. "You didn't fall for that stuff, did you? It's standard campfire scare tactics. Pure cheese."

"I'm not stupid," she snapped. "I just don't like jokes about Luthor being in danger."

At first, the woods were full of the other teams, counting off paces and following their instruction sheets. But as they got farther from the camp, the crowd began to thin out. They were trying out an over-grown path that Griffin had noticed that morning, hoping it might be a shortcut to Luthor's cabin, one that bypassed the shore route.

"I'm pretty sure this is it," Griffin announced. "If we keep going straight—"

The snapping of a twig behind them made them jump.

"Is someone there?" Savannah demanded. There was no answer.

"We heard you," Griffin announced. "Show yourself."

A stocky figure stepped out from behind a bramble, grinning wolfishly. "Wow, how about this Cedarville reunion right up here at Ebony Lake!"

"Vader!" Griffin seethed. "I should have known it would be you! Where's your orienteering partner?"

Darren shrugged. "I ditched him. I'm not much of a compass jockey. I'm more interested in other stuff—like what you meant when you said, 'If we keep going straight.' What are you looking for, Bing? What are you guys up to?"

"We're orienteering, like you're supposed to be," Savannah retorted.

"Yeah, right. You don't even have a compass."

"Sure we do." Griffin reached into his pocket for the instrument. What he drew out instead was a Puppy Treat he had brought for Luthor.

Darren's eyes bulged. "Is that a *dog biscuit*?"

"This? Of course not! It's a high protein bar!" There were moments, Griffin knew, when a sacrifice had to be made in order to protect the plan. This was one of those moments. Without hesitation, he popped the bone-shaped cookie into his mouth, chewed, and swallowed, stifling his gag reflex. The thing tasted meaty, like the way he remembered liver. "It's awesome," he managed. "Lots of fiber, too."

"Darren!" came an annoyed voice from the woods. Marty appeared amid the trees. "What are you doing? Scotty's all the way back by the boulders. Come on. The clock's ticking."

"Well, what about these guys?" Darren asked in annoyance. "They're not doing it right, either."

"Yeah, but you're not doing it at all. Let's go." He waved to Griffin and Savannah. "You guys okay?"

Griffin waved back. "We'll figure it out. Bye, Darren."

And the counselor left, with Darren in tow.

Now that Darren was out of the picture, they were free to follow the overgrown path. Sure enough, it led to the shore just west of Luthor's cabin. Still tethered to the long rope, the Doberman came out to greet them, and there was another joyous reunion with Savannah.

Savannah unhooked the leash from the pump handle, and Luthor galloped and played like a small puppy. At one point, he mistook the flat expanse of lake for an open plane, and was the most surprised creature on earth to find himself swimming instead of running.

He was less excited by the idea of being tethered to the leash again. Even Savannah's dog-whispering wasn't quite convincing enough. His canine brain was having trouble understanding the purpose of this strange place that had no houses and no cars, and was so unlike home. But there was Savannah, and there was food, and that was all he'd ever needed before.

Leery of a second Darren sighting, they took the lakeside route back to camp. They were approaching the beach, inventing stories for what had gone wrong with their orienteering, when a small powerboat came in close to shore. The driver cut the motor and anchored the craft close to where they stood. He swung a leg over the side and dropped into the knee-deep water, protected by high hip waders.

"A little off course, aren't you?" he asked in a friendly tone. "Everybody else is way over on the other side."

Griffin shrugged. "Maybe *they're* lost."

The young man looked startled for a moment, and then threw back his head and laughed. "Maybe," he agreed. He was probably in his late twenties, with a manner that instantly put both campers at their ease. He opened a belt pack of small vials and began to collect samples from the lake. "Malachi Moore. Pleased to meet you. I'm with the Inland Freshwater Research Institute — you know, the squints across the lake."

"I'm Griffin, and this is Savannah."

Malachi placed the filled bottles into a small box. "So what do you two do for fun around here, besides not orienteering?"

"The usual camp stuff, I guess," Griffin replied.

"What about you? What do you do for fun at the institute?"

"Oh, it's a barrel of laughs. We check our water samples for bacterial levels and acid rain. And we're on a first-name basis with a whole lot of fish."

"Hey, you two—" Head counselor Cyrus emerged from the woods. "You're totally off the map. I thought we were going to have to send out a search party."

"Sorry," said Savannah, chastened. A search party was the last thing they needed, with Luthor hiding out here.

"Some of it's my fault," Malachi admitted. "I was chewing their ears off about my fascinating life hanging out with eighty-year-old scientists." He held out his hand. "Malachi Moore, from the institute."

The two campers and the head counselor wound up riding back to their camp dock in Malachi's boat. As it turned out, Cyrus and the researcher had both grown up in the Baltimore suburbs, and talked endlessly about "the old neighborhood," and whether or not the Ravens had the stuff to make it to the Super Bowl. Griffin was grateful for any distraction from the subject of what had drawn two campers more than a mile away from the orienteering route.

About halfway home, they could clearly hear the distant barking of a large canine.

Savannah shut her eyes and tried to will Luthor into silence. Her dog-whispering, though, didn't work from remote locations.

"Is that a wolf?" asked Malachi.

Cyrus frowned. "We had a strange incident with an animal while one of our buses was unloading."

"It's a great view from out here," Griffin said in an effort to change the subject.

It was going to be a really long month.

9

When Griffin emerged from Cabin 14 in an oversized Care Bears T-shirt, even Savannah laughed.

"Considering it was your dog who ate all my stuff," he said, tight-lipped, "I think I should get a little more respect from you!"

"I know! I'm sorry!" Savannah giggled. "But — Care Bears?"

"Marty got it from the lost and found. It was either this or a Mets shirt, and no self-respecting Yankee fan would ever wear that!"

Large grills sizzled all around the compound, and the air was fragrant with cooking smoke. Hamburgers and hot dogs were on the menu, and hungry campers waited impatiently for dinner to be ready.

"Let's put away a few burgers for Luthor," Savannah whispered. "I don't want to run out of dog food."

In line at the grill, they found none other than Malachi Moore helping out, making friends, and serving food.

"Cyrus invited me," he explained, handing Griffin and Savannah a hot dog each. "He took pity on me and spared me a night of staring at protozoa through a microscope."

"Care Bears, huh, Bing?" came Darren Vader's nasal voice. "Should have known you were a fan."

Griffin took a bite of his hot dog. "Beat it, Vader."

"Okay. Maybe I'll check my e-mail from back home. You learn a lot of interesting things about Cedarville when you're not there."

Griffin frowned. "Like what?"

"Well, my mom said that guy Swindle's back in town," Darren offered. "He came for his dog. But — funny thing — the mutt's missing. How wild is that?"

"Swindle doesn't *have* a dog!" Savannah burst out. "Luthor is mine! And he *is* missing!"

"Seems to me you're not that broken up about it," Darren observed. "Maybe you know something I don't know." He paused. "And maybe I know the thing you think I don't know."

"What are you trying to say?" Griffin demanded.

Darren's expression was as unpleasant as it had ever been. "Remember the mysterious animal that attacked our bus driver? Remember the dog biscuit you tried to pass off as an energy bar? I'm saying the pooch is closer than we think. You're hiding him up here somewhere. So what's in it for me if I *don't* e-mail that information back to Cedarville?"

"What is it you think you can get out of us?"

Savannah asked, mystified. "All we have is our clothes, and Griffin doesn't even have that!"

"Money," said Darren firmly. "And maybe an iPod if you guys have one of the good ones that does Skype."

"Oh," said Griffin sarcastically. "In that case, I'll give you a million dollars! Because I'm a billionaire— at least I am in your deranged fantasyland where I'm hiding a dog at summer camp! Get a grip, Vader! This is too stupid, even for you!"

"Did you hear that barking today?" Darren asked innocently. "Sounded like a big dog—maybe a Doberman."

Griffin and Savannah held an emergency meeting by the bathroom station.

"I knew the minute Vader stepped on that bus that he was trouble!" Griffin raged.

"But what are we going to *do*?" Savannah pleaded. "He *knows* about Luthor!"

"As long as he thinks he can get something out of it, he isn't going to tell anybody," Griffin assured her. "We'll string him along, keep his hopes alive that he can blackmail us. The plan is still on track. We just have to stay cool."

They circulated from grill to grill, collecting hot dogs and burgers to take to Luthor after the camp had gone to sleep. His pockets stuffed with meat, Griffin returned to Bunk 14 to stash the dog's dinner. But as he approached the darkened cabin, instinct made him stop on the threshold.

Someone was in there, someone with a flashlight.

"Hello?" He turned on the lights to reveal Malachi Moore, down on one knee, peering under a bed.

The young researcher jumped up. "Griffin — you startled me!"

"What are you doing in our cabin?" Griffin blurted.

"Is this your cabin? I was actually looking for the bathroom."

For a scientist, Malachi wasn't a very good liar. No one looked for a bathroom underneath a bunk bed.

"You need the wash station," Griffin told him, "that big building in the center of all the cabins. The boys' side is facing us."

"Thanks," said Malachi, and he walked out, leaving Griffin with his mind in a whirl. What could a researcher at an institute possibly be looking for at a kids' camp? Was he just a sneak thief? Or could he be something more sinister than that?

Griffin was sure he had discovered something important. But what?

After dinner, Cyrus introduced Malachi to the assembled campers.

"This is Dr. Moore, who works at the Inland Freshwater Research Institute across the lake. He's going to arrange for us to tour the lab and be their guests for lunch."

There was thunderous applause. The facility tour would be a nice change, but the break from camp food was the real crowd-pleaser.

"I don't trust that guy," Griffin muttered.

"Malachi?" repeated Savannah in surprise. "He's nice."

"I just caught him poking around my cabin. He said he was looking for the bathroom."

She shrugged. "It's not impossible."

"On the floor under my bunk?"

Savannah tried to be reasonable. "We've been dealing with so many sleazoids lately—first Swindle, then Vader. I'm so worried about Luthor I can barely think straight. Maybe we're both being a little paranoid."

"Maybe," mumbled Griffin. But he did not seem convinced.

From: Griffin
To: Melissa
What can you find out about Malachi Moore,
scientist at the Inland Freshwater Research
Institute? Need ASAP.

From: Melissa
To: Griffin
No Malachi Moore employed by Institute. Checked
support staff, too. Don't know who this guy is. Be
careful.

10

Griffin Bing wasn't the only man with a plan.

Darren Vader was up before anyone else the next morning, tiptoeing out of Bunk 14, pausing only to drape a dirty sweat sock over the sleeping Griffin's toothbrush.

Eat my feet, Bing, he thought triumphantly. After this morning's work, Griffin would be eating Darren's dust, too.

The sun had just barely put in an appearance, peeking out between dark gray clouds. Camp was deserted when Darren rambled across the compound. He headed east into the woods, looking for the overgrown path he'd traveled yesterday, following Griffin and Savannah. He was positive they'd hidden the dog out here somewhere. But he needed to be able to prove it.

That was his strategy. If Drysdale and Bing were too cheap to pay him for his silence, then he'd go straight to Swindle, who'd be so grateful that he'd offer a generous reward. Come to think of it, Darren liked that idea even better. An adult had more money than a couple of kids.

At last, he found the path and began to follow it. The weeds were a little wet from an early-morning shower, but the big rain was holding off so far. Perfect conditions for a walk while you planned what you were going to do with all the cash you were going to get. He kept his eyes peeled right and left. He wasn't certain what he was looking for, but there would probably be a shelter of some kind, like a cave, or maybe a little hut.

His confidence began to fade when he saw that he was approaching the lake. Had he missed it somehow? But no, there it was — a cabin, weather-beaten, low to the ground, almost consumed by vegetation.

Something clicked in his mind. That stupid story about the mechanical monster — this had to be the place Cyrus was talking about, where that nutjob ate his fishy friend and replaced him with spare parts. Maybe some of that dumb story was true. Either way, it didn't matter. There was no money in stories. Show dogs, on the other hand . . .

He approached the structure and threw open the rickety door. "Hey, mutt, there's a new sheriff in —!"

The roar that came from Luthor rattled everything in Darren's head. There was the scrambling of toenails on wood flooring, and then the Doberman was airborne, a black-and-brown shape growing ever larger in the intruder's field of vision.

Darren had only a split second to contemplate the two things he knew about this huge, ferocious animal: (1) the dog was fiercely loyal to Drysdale, and (2) anyone Drysdale didn't like, Luthor probably wasn't too fond of, either.

He ran, propelled by a terror far greater than anything he had ever known. Behind him, there was a tremendous crash, and Luthor exploded out the door, hauling behind him the broken top of an iron water pump. It smashed the door frame as it blasted through, swinging wildly at the other end of the dog's leash. The pump looked heavy, but it wasn't slowing the Doberman down.

Darren Vader had never been able to climb a tree in his life. But he went up this one, howling even louder than the animal that pursued him. He cowered on a branch, just a few inches above those slavering, snapping jaws.

The minute Griffin woke up, he could tell there was something wrong. "What's going on?" he blurted.

Marty peered in the front door. "Has anyone seen Darren this morning?"

Griffin understood instantly. Vader, that lowlife, that snail slime, was looking for Luthor. In a whirlwind, he scrambled into his clothes and ran out of the cabin. He very nearly tripped over Savannah, who was waiting for him, nearly hysterical.

"Darren's missing! I'm *positive* he's gone after Luthor!"

Griffin nodded seriously. "We've got to go find him."

"I don't care if Darren Vader falls off the edge of the earth!" Savannah exclaimed savagely. "It's Luthor I'm worried about!"

"Think!" he ordered. "If we can't bring Darren back fast, the counselors will search every inch of the woods. They'll find Vader *and* Luthor, and the whole plan will be down the drain."

Savannah looked frantic. "There are dozens of them, and only two of us!"

"But we have an advantage," he reminded her. "We know where we're going."

They slipped out unnoticed amid the chaos of the camp, and raced into the woods, turning right at the overgrown path that was now familiar to them. As they ran, distant sounds became more distinct—the barking of an angry dog and a plaintive human voice yelling for help.

"If Darren's done anything to harm Luthor—" Savannah began.

That wasn't how Griffin interpreted what he was hearing. But he realized it didn't matter who was winning and who wasn't. From the perspective of the plan, Luthor hurting Darren was just as bad as Darren hurting Luthor. Both would bring attention to a fugitive dog and a violated court order. The only winner would be Swindle.

When Griffin and Savannah arrived on the scene, the sight that met their eyes was almost comical—

Luthor, leaping and snapping at the dangling Darren while dragging around the remnants of the broken pump.

Savannah dropped down on one knee and gathered her beloved dog into her arms. "It's all right, sweetie. I won't let him hurt you."

"Are you blind?" Darren shrieked, clinging to the branch as if his life depended on it. *"Me* hurt *him*? Which one of us is in the tree? He tried to kill me!"

"If you survive," Savannah said coldly, "it'll be because *I* didn't kill you, not Luthor!"

"You can blame each other later," Griffin said briskly. "But right now every counselor at Ebony Lake is out looking for this dimwit. The sooner we get him back to camp, the safer Luthor's going to be."

"I'm afraid it's not going to work out that way," came a voice from behind them.

11

G riffin and Savannah wheeled around.

Malachi Moore stepped out of a stand of birch trees and approached them, carrying a pistol-sized tranquilizer gun.

Spying the weapon, Savannah stepped in front of Luthor.

"Oh, I'm not going to hurt him," Malachi assured her in a friendly tone. "It's just a tranquilizer dart — you know, to make it easier to get him back to Mr. Palomino."

Griffin's eyes bulged. "You work for *Swindle*?"

Malachi grinned appreciatively. "Nice nickname. I don't like him much, either. But business is business. Sorry, guys."

At that moment, Darren lost his shaky grip on the branch and dropped like a stone to the forest floor.

Startled, Malachi turned and looked down at the fallen boy. "Are you okay?"

Savannah knew she'd never get another chance. She

picked up the pump handle at the end of Luthor's leash and swung it with all her might, slamming it across Malachi's shoulders. He collapsed to the ground, stunned.

"Run!" bellowed The Man With The Plan.

He began to scuttle along the overgrown path in the direction they'd come. Savannah untangled Luthor's leash from the broken pump and followed.

Darren scrambled to his feet. "Wait for me!"

Luthor halted him in his tracks with an angry bark.

"Don't even think about it, Vader!" Griffin rasped. "This is all your fault!"

Darren was the picture of innocence. "It's my fault Swindle hired a goon to kidnap the dog?" He indicated Malachi, who was dazed and barely moving.

"If you weren't such a greedy, blackmailing slime-bucket, you would have stayed in your bunk instead of coming for Luthor!" Savannah accused. "Then the whole camp wouldn't be searching for you right now! For all of us, probably!"

"And *this* guy couldn't have followed you," Griffin added resentfully, gesturing toward the prostrate form of Swindle's hired man. "Which is *totally messing up the plan*!"

"How do you know he didn't follow *you*?" Darren shot back.

With a groan, Malachi rolled over.

"Let's get out of here!" Savannah hissed.

With a silent nod, Griffin continued along the trail,

noting in annoyance that Darren was tagging along at a safe distance behind the Doberman. Too bad rescuing Luthor also meant bailing out this big jerk.

Calm down, he thought. The important thing was getting Luthor away from Swindle's hired gun.

All at once, he froze.

"Why are we stopping?" asked Savannah.

"Shhhh!" Griffin put a finger to his lips. There were voices in the forest — not just a few — accompanied by the rustle and snap of footfalls through the underbrush.

"The counselors!" Savannah whispered in alarm. She aimed an accusing finger at Darren. "Looking for *him*!"

"If they find me, I'll tell them about the mutt," Darren threatened.

Savannah was distraught. "What are we going to do?"

Griffin started back toward the cabin. "To the lake!"

Darren was astounded. *"That's* your plan? To swim for it?"

"There's an old rowboat by the shore." It rankled Griffin to have to explain his reasoning to his worst enemy. But if he couldn't get Darren to shut his mouth, the searchers would be upon them in a matter of minutes. "The counselors will be checking the woods, not the water. Maybe they won't notice us."

The four of them — Griffin, Savannah, Darren, and Luthor — doubled back along the path toward the shoreline. They tiptoed a wide berth around Malachi, who was stirring like someone waking after a long sleep. They didn't dare slow down, though. The counselors' voices in the woods seemed to be growing louder.

As they passed Luthor's cabin, the ground became softer, marshier. Griffin knew the water couldn't be far now. All at once, the heavy bushes parted to reveal the glassy black expanse of Ebony Lake. On the beach, just a few yards down, was the rowboat.

When Griffin tried to pull the small craft into the water, he got a nasty shock. The weathered hull wouldn't budge. The years had mired it deep into the sand and silt. He dropped to his knees and began to scrabble at the sediment and mud.

"Come on," he whispered urgently. "Help me get this thing out!"

"Dream on, Bing," Darren sneered. "I'm not taking a slime bath for you or anybody."

But a threatening growl from Luthor had him down on all fours, breaking up the ground under the wooden boat. Savannah worked beside him. Even the Doberman clued in and devoted his considerable digging skills to the task, sending showers of gritty sludge onto his three human partners.

"Easy, Fido!" sputtered Darren, spitting sand. "You're not burying a bone here!"

"Luthor does not eat bones," Savannah informed him, panting a little. "His meals are nutritionally balanced and veterinarian recommended."

"Less fighting and more working," Griffin urged. "The counselors will be on us any second!"

A dollop of wet mud struck Darren in the eye, and he leaped upright. "You're not the boss of me, Bing! Let's see how you like being muck-bombed by a giant mutt!" In a fit of rage, he reared back his leg and delivered a vicious kick to the wooden hull.

The boat *moved.*

O w!" Darren collapsed to the beach, cradling his foot.

Griffin and Savannah ignored him. Grunting from the strain, they hauled the small craft out of its prison of sand and dragged it into the shallow water.

"Will it even float?" Savannah asked anxiously.

It was a good question. After decades entombed in the damp earth of the shore, parts of the wood were dark with weakness and rot. Griffin peered into the curved bottom. It seemed dry enough. He stepped aboard. His shoe did not break clear through the hull. No leaking water pooled at his feet.

"Seems seaworthy. Come on!" He helped Savannah over the gunwale, and Luthor leaped on board after her. The rowboat pitched dangerously from the Doberman's weight, then stabilized. "Let's go, Vader."

Darren was still writhing on the beach. "I'm injured!"

"Can't we just leave him?" Savannah pleaded.

"Good idea," Griffin announced in a stage whisper aimed at Darren. "We can't risk getting caught for a jerk like him." He leaned over the side and began a dog-paddle motion in the water. The boat inched away from the beach.

"Hey, no fair!" The big boy splashed through the shallows and half climbed, half dove aboard the craft. Luthor let out a cry of outrage as Darren came down on his hindquarters. Terrified, the new arrival fell over, bumped heads with Griffin, and landed flat on his face in the wooden bottom. All that action served to send the rowboat drifting out into the lake.

There were no oars, so they paddled with their hands. Their escape was slow at first. But when they coordinated the rhythm of their strokes, the small craft began to make progress away from the shore.

"Don't stop!" Griffin said harshly when Darren's efforts slackened. "If any of those counselors hits the beach, we need to be a tiny dot halfway across the lake."

They were about eighty yards out when the first of the searchers emerged from the cover of the trees. It was Cyrus.

"Get down!" Griffin hissed.

He ducked, pulling Darren along with him. Savannah leaned over Luthor's sleek back, gentling the two of them below the level of the gunwale.

"Don't touch me!" Darren snapped irritably, shaking himself free of Griffin. But he remained out of sight.

Staying flat, Griffin peered over the side. Cyrus

had been joined by Marty, the Cabin 14 counselor. They gazed intently along the shoreline, but glanced only briefly out at the lake. If they noticed the rowboat riding low in the black water, they gave no sign. After another brief but urgent conversation, they disappeared into the woods to continue the search.

Savannah was amazed. "Didn't they see us? Surely they spotted the boat, at least."

Griffin allowed himself to resume breathing. "They're not looking for a boat. They're looking for a missing kid."

"But we can't just float around the lake forever," Savannah pointed out. "Sooner or later, we'll have to go back."

"We can wait them out," Griffin reasoned. "Eventually, they'll call off the hunt and contact the police, or the forest service, or whoever's in charge out here. That's when we stash the dog someplace new, and wander in with a story about how we took a walk in the woods and got lost. They'll be mad, but we'll cry all over the place about how scared we were and how sorry we are."

"You know, Bing," Darren said with grudging respect, "I used to think you were a moron. But there might be something to these dumb plans of yours after all."

Savannah was disgusted. "I should have expected you to be impressed by something dishonest and sleazy."

"Like you're too high and mighty to go along with it," Darren sneered.

"Only for my sweetie," she replied primly, massaging the fur at the base of Luthor's sturdy neck. "I'd do anything to protect him."

That was when they heard the motor.

A sleek shape was tearing across the lake from the direction of the abandoned cabin. It was a powerboat, coming up fast. Griffin squinted at the face behind the windscreen.

"Malachi!" Savannah exclaimed in horror.

Griffin bent double over the bow and began to paddle wildly. "Evasive action!"

Savannah tried to form a makeshift oar with both hands, stroking with all her might.

"You're wasting your time," scoffed Darren. "No way can you outrun a motorboat."

As much as Griffin hated to agree with Darren, this time his old enemy was right. They were wallowing in the water, sitting ducks. Swindle's agent was screaming down on them — on a collision course with the small craft.

"Is he going to ram us?" Savannah quavered in terror.

"He can't risk anything happening to Luthor," Griffin blustered, wishing he sounded more convinced.

"It's all Drysdale's fault!" Darren raged.

"*My* fault?"

"You're the one who conked the guy with that pump

handle and made him mad! And now he's going to sink us!"

No one was paddling any longer. The four occupants of the ancient dory—human and canine—watched in horror as the speedboat bore down on them. It was now close enough for Griffin to read the grim determination in Malachi's eyes. Swindle's man wasn't stopping. Impact was mere seconds away.

"Hang on!" Griffin cried, waiting for the racing craft to close the final thirty feet between them.

Without warning, a large, bulbous, silver-and-black form broke the surface directly in the path of the hurtling motorboat.

Darren's eyes nearly popped out of their sockets. "The mechanical monster of Ebony Lake!" he shrieked.

13

Griffin and Savannah gawked in amazement at the bizarre metal object — creature? — that had appeared out of nowhere from the depths of the lake.

To Malachi, the strange machine represented something far more urgent than any old legend. It was an enormous obstacle several times the size of the motorboat. And it was *directly in his path!*

He twirled the wheel in a desperate attempt to avoid the contraption. Yet, unlike a car, a watercraft does not respond instantly to steering. He veered to port too late. There was a loud bang as the starboard side of the motorboat smashed into the much larger object. It ricocheted off like a Ping-Pong ball, flipped over, and landed in the water upside down. A moment later, Malachi Moore popped up to the surface a few feet away from his capsized vessel, floundering and calling for help.

A very unlikely hero came to his aid. Luthor leaped out of the rowboat and hit the water with a titanic splash. Paddling confidently, the big Doberman swam over to the man who'd been hired to abduct him. Malachi latched on to Luthor's collar and allowed himself to be towed to the dory. Griffin and Savannah worked together to haul rescuer and castaway aboard.

Darren was beside himself. "You can't save him! He's the enemy!"

Griffin was disgusted. "What do you want us to do — let him drown?"

Savannah beamed at Luthor. "I've never been so proud of you as I am right now, sweetie. He didn't deserve your compassion, but you gave it to him anyway — because it was the *human* thing to do."

Luthor shook himself, drenching everybody who wasn't already drenched.

"But the *monster* —" Darren could not wrest his attention from the gleaming behemoth that had appeared from the depths of the lake and knocked out Malachi's powerboat.

"There's no such thing — *yikes!*" Griffin swallowed his own words as the bobbing machine swung around in the water to reveal a huge, translucent eye.

Savannah gasped in disbelief. Even Malachi recoiled with shock. Luthor let out a low growl, but it was a cautious growl. He was no longer the alpha dog in the presence of this larger metallic newcomer.

Griffin peered into the terrifying eyeball and saw —

"A person?" he blurted in amazement.

Griffin stared into the thick glass. A woman wearing a headset was looking out at him. And there was someone beside her — a man, working at an instrument panel.

"The mechanical monster of Ebony Lake is — a *submarine*?" managed Savannah.

"But who needs a submarine in a lake?" Darren demanded.

"Researchers do," Malachi supplied in a weary voice.

That was when Griffin caught sight of the markings on the "monster's" side: INLAND FRESHWATER RESEARCH INSTITUTE.

"It's the scientists across the lake!" he exclaimed in wonder.

"All these years, people have been spotting the mechanical monster from that crazy story," Savannah marveled. "And *this* is what it really was."

"Yeah," Darren snorted. "How dumb can you get? I wasn't fooled for a second."

"Not for a second," Griffin agreed sarcastically. "That's why you practically laid an egg when that thing appeared."

"I did not!"

The door of the sub hissed open, and the woman stepped out onto the running board. "Everybody okay here?" she called in concern. Her gaze fixed on Malachi, who was hunched over, rubbing the back of his neck. "Maybe we should get you to a doctor. That was quite a collision."

"I'm not hurting from the collision," Malachi tried to explain. "I'm hurting from when *she* tried to smash my head in with a—" He turned to Savannah. "What *was* that?"

"A pump handle," she told him. "And I'll do it again if you go anywhere near my dog."

"Kid, I wouldn't touch your dog now," Malachi said sincerely. "He saved my life." He reached over to pet Luthor, and just barely escaped with all his fingers attached.

The other scientist appeared behind his partner. "Catch." He heaved a coil of rope across the water. Griffin caught it deftly. "Tie yourself on, and we'll tow you home. We'd bring you aboard with us, but there's not enough room in the submersible."

"I assume you're from the camp over there," the woman added. She glared disapprovingly at Malachi. "I hope you're not the counselor in charge of boating safety."

"He's not a counselor," said Savannah through clenched teeth. "He's a hired goon."

"Retired," amended Malachi. "I'm harmless now. Scout's honor."

There was a brief discussion about what to do with the powerboat. That question answered itself, though, when the overturned craft tipped up and slipped beneath the surface of Ebony Lake without so much as a gurgle.

"Mr. Palomino's not going to like that," Malachi

commented, still rubbing his neck. "The rental was on his credit card."

In the face of a plan gone awry, it was the one piece of news that could have brought a smile to Griffin's lips. To Swindle, the only thing worse than failure was a failure that cost him money.

"There's one thing I can't understand," Griffin wondered. "How did Swindle figure out what camp we'd be going to?"

Malachi shrugged. "He knew where the dog lived. All he had to do was search the mailbox until he saw a notice from Ebony Lake. Not the nicest guy in the world, but he's pretty sharp. I'd hate to have him as an enemy."

"Tell me about it," groaned Griffin.

They were a bizarre spectacle as they moved slowly toward shore — a gleaming high-tech submersible towing an ancient wooden rowboat at a speed that barely created a wake. After the wild, crazed action of the past hour, it felt to Griffin like being put into suspended animation.

A distant ringing jolted everyone back to reality.

"It's mine." Malachi reached into his jacket pocket and produced a cell phone in a waterproof pouch. "It's my boss — my *ex*-boss." He slipped the handset out of its protector. "Hi, Mr. Palomino . . . yeah, the dog's right here. Hey, Luthor — say woof."

The Doberman growled as if he knew who was on the other end of the line.

"No, I definitely won't be bringing him today . . . When? How about never? The big fellow saved my life. So I owe him."

Malachi held the phone away from his ear. The other occupants of the craft could hear enraged ranting coming from the other end of the line.

Griffin stifled an impulse to call out something nasty. For all he knew, Swindle might be recording the conversation. The guy had already figured out who took the dog. No sense giving him proof he could present to the judge. Then they'd be the ones who'd have to go into hiding, not just Luthor.

"Malachi quit, but that doesn't mean *we* can't do business!" Darren shouted at the phone. "My name is Darren Va—"

The Doberman silenced him with an eardrum-cracking bark at point-blank range. Darren recoiled abruptly and very nearly toppled out of the rowboat and into the lake.

"Anyway," Malachi continued into the handset, "I wish I could say it was a pleasure doing business with you, but it wasn't. Oh—and sorry about the rent-a-boat. It sleeps with the fishes." He clicked off.

By this time, they could make out the camp dock and the frenzied activity in the compound. The search was probably still in full swing—for three campers now, not just one.

It was clear to Griffin that this part of the plan had

been taken as far as it could go. He caught Savannah's eye and mouthed the words: "Code Z."

It brought instant understanding. Every operation had a Code Z built into it. It was the escape clause—the moment when all that remained was to get the heck out of there, regroup, and try to save the pieces, if there were any.

Savannah returned a barely noticeable nod of agreement. She curled her fingers under Luthor's collar, and she and Griffin counted silently:

One . . . two . . . *three!*

Griffin, Savannah, and the Doberman bounded overboard and hit the surface of the lake swimming.

14

"Come back, you guys!" Malachi shouted after them. The cold of the water knifed through them, energizing tired arms and legs. They stroked for shore in a path that would land them well away from the camp beach.

"Honest, I quit!" Swindle's man persisted. "And I lost the dart gun anyway!"

Griffin and Savannah had already moved on to the next challenge. Maybe they no longer had anything to fear from Malachi, but what about Cyrus and the counselors? If Camp Ebony Lake were to discover that a fugitive dog was being harbored there, Griffin and Savannah would be sent home, and Luthor with them—straight into Swindle's ruthless, money-grubbing clutches.

"You stink, Bing!" Darren bellowed. "I'm not going to take the heat for this alone! I'm going to rat you out—you and your stupid dog!"

"He'll do it, too," Savannah moaned, freestyling next to Luthor.

"Keep swimming," Griffin panted back. "I can only plan when I'm on dry land!"

Within minutes of grueling effort, Griffin was wishing he'd declared the Code Z a little closer to shore. The Doberman could easily have been on the beach already, but he never left Savannah's side, paddling tirelessly.

At last, the three staggered onto the sand, gasping.

Savannah would not let her exhaustion interfere with the urgent need for action. "What now?"

"We re-hide the dog," Griffin decided. "Then back to camp for damage control."

"Damage control?" she echoed. "Darren's going to tell them about Luthor!"

"Maybe no one will believe him. He's in pretty deep trouble right now. Who knows? He might even keep his mouth shut. There's a first time for everything. Remember, this doesn't make him look so great, either."

They found a temporary spot for Luthor in the woods—a natural half alcove formed by a low ledge of rock. Savannah slipped the end of the leash around a narrow birch trunk.

"We'll be back for you soon, sweetie," Savannah promised. "*Real* soon."

The normally antsy Doberman seemed satisfied with that. He curled up in his niche, grateful for the chance to rest. Already that day, he'd busted out of an old cabin, dislodged the handle from an iron pump, treed Darren, rescued Malachi, and dog-paddled a million miles of lake. That had to count as a big morning, even for Luthor.

It was a miserable walk back to camp. Griffin and Savannah's wet clothes were heavy and uncomfortable, and their sneakers squished with every step. The forest bugs found their condition especially appealing.

Savannah swatted at a swarm of gnats. "How are we supposed to explain the fact that we're soaked to the skin?"

"We'll have to sneak into our cabins and change before the counselors see us," Griffin replied. "I hope Marty hooked me up with some new Care Bears gear. Maybe I'll get lucky, and it'll be Teletubbies this time."

"Big joke," she mumbled, and was instantly sorry. What would she and Luthor have done without Griffin's brave heart and level head? He was The Man With The Plan, even in the face of disaster. But this looked like the end of the road — and not just for her poor dog. That horrible S. Wendell Palomino was out to get all of them eventually.

They broke through the trees and ran out into the large clearing that held the buildings and playing fields of Camp Ebony Lake. The hope of getting to their cabins unobserved popped like a bubble. Darren stood with Cyrus and Marty in the center of the compound, shooting his mouth off—a long story, complete with hand gestures, obviously in great detail. The Oscar-winning performance concluded with Darren's finger pointed directly at Griffin and Savannah.

Griffin groaned. "If you look up 'tattletale' on Wikipedia, there should be a video clip of that."

Savannah wasn't laughing. "This is no time for jokes! How are we going to protect Luthor *now*?"

The Man With The Plan took a deep breath. "We'll say Vader's lying. He's always lying—why should today be any different?"

"But the counselors are going to know he's telling the truth when they see how wet we are!" she shrilled.

"We could tell them we got all sweaty . . ." he offered lamely.

"Oh, come on, Griffin! We don't need dumb excuses; we need a miracle!"

There was a loud clap of thunder and the heavens opened up with the storm that had been brewing all morning. The downpour was so intense that they could barely see each other, much less Darren and the counselors a hundred yards away.

"Ha!" Griffin was triumphant. "That's why we're wet—we got caught in the rain like everybody else! I hate to admit it, but there are times when no plan is a substitute for plain dumb luck!"

They laughed as they ran, not because it was funny, but from the sheer release of tension. When at last they came staggering into the cover of the mess hall, they found most of the camp already there, sheltering from the storm, just as drenched as they were.

Cyrus rushed forward, his brow almost as dark as the thunderheads outside. "Where have you two been?"

Griffin cast him a look of newborn innocence. "We were looking for Darren, but we got turned around in the woods. It was pretty scary." It was technically the truth—with a few important details left out.

"Liar!" Darren exploded. "You've got a dog out there, and it attacked me! But then Malachi drove his boat into the mechanical monster, which is really a submarine! And then you guys jumped in the lake!" He turned to Cyrus. "Look how soaked they are!"

"We're all soaked," the head counselor said in exasperation. "Darren, I want you to go see Nurse McNulty. You had a pretty stressful morning. You'd better get some rest this afternoon."

"I'm not stressed—I'm telling the truth!" Darren pleaded. "It's not my fault it sounds like lies!"

"Come on, Darren," Griffin chided. "Who takes a dog to summer camp?"

Huddled under a vast umbrella, Marty bundled Darren—still protesting and accusing—off to the infirmary. When the screen door slapped shut behind them, Cyrus fixed Griffin with a piercing gaze. "The next time I see Malachi, he's not going to know anything about all this, right?"

"Of course not," Griffin replied readily.

"Besides," Savannah added, "I don't think he'll be

coming by here anymore. The last time I saw him, he said something about quitting his job."

When the rain finally abated, and Griffin made it back to Cabin 14, he found fresh clothes folded on his bunk. The T-shirt featured a black-and-white photograph of a kissing bride and groom inside a heart-shaped frame of pink and red roses. The caption read: *Marco and Elyse, Endless Love, May 11, 1999.*

"Is this a step up from Care Bears?"

Startled, Griffin whipped around to see Marty standing in the doorway. "It's dry," he replied. "That's definitely an improvement. Thanks."

"Anytime." The counselor regarded him intently. "You know, Griffin, when you first got here—when your stuff was all torn up—I remember thinking it looked like it had been chewed by some kind of animal. That couldn't have had anything to do with a dog, could it?"

"I was thinking more of a Nile crocodile," Griffin joked. "Or maybe a velociraptor."

Marty laughed. But, Griffin reflected, there was nothing funny about the conversation. It wasn't his first clue that Luthor was no longer safe at Ebony Lake. But it was the one that put things over the top.

"The good news is Cyrus and Marty don't believe Darren," he told Savannah at an emergency meeting behind the wash station while the other campers were at lunch. "The bad news is they don't really believe *us,* either. At least, they're suspicious that there's something going on behind their backs."

"My counselor hasn't taken her eyes of me since we got back," Savannah reported mournfully. "It's like the whole camp is on high alert for anything out of the ordinary."

"The next time the counselors hear barking, it won't be *'oh, hey, what's that?'*" Griffin agreed. "They'll turn the world upside down until somebody stumbles on Luthor."

"Or they'll follow *us* sneaking out to see him, which is just as bad," Savannah added.

Griffin's expression was grave. "It's not just the counselors I'm worried about. Malachi told Swindle we were hiding the dog, so Swindle knows Luthor's location. He can't stay here anymore."

Savannah was appalled. "He *has* to stay here! Where else can he go?"

"I think I might know a place," said The Man With The Plan.

15

From: Griffin
To: Melissa
Urgent. Operation compromised. Need to move
package. Can you and Logan keep at Camp Ta-da!
till heat's off . . . ?

Melissa stared at the small screen of her phone in disbelief. Was he talking about *Luthor*? What else could the "package" possibly be?

Melissa was afraid of Luthor. Scared to death, actually. She accepted Savannah's word that the Doberman was sweet and loving at his core. But since Savannah was the only person who could reach Luthor's core, that wasn't much use to anyone else.

"How's this?"

Logan stood on the edge of the stage in Camp Ta-da!'s performance center, his face illuminated by a single brilliant spotlight. For the past hour, he had been adjusting the beam a millimeter or two this way and that, and demanding her opinion.

"Fine," she told him. "It was fine an hour ago, too. To be honest, Logan, I can't really tell the difference."

He glared at her. "I have what is known in the theatre as a 'needle nose.' If the lighting isn't exactly perfect, it looks wrong. Whole careers have crashed and burned because some stage manager made an actor's nose look too big, or too small, or too bulbous, or too needly—"

"I get it." It wasn't like shy Melissa to interrupt, but the text from Camp Ebony Lake was weighing heavily on her mind. "Listen, we just got an emergency message from Griffin and Savannah. They want to know if we can hide Luthor here for a while."

Logan did a double take. "Are you crazy? That dog's a lethal weapon! And besides, how are we supposed to get him here all the way from Ebony Lake?"

She shrugged. "It's only twenty-five miles. If anyone can make it happen, Griffin can. They wouldn't ask if it wasn't important."

"It doesn't matter," Logan shot back. "Ta-da! is a drama camp. Maybe your parents only sent you here to bring you out of your shell, but acting is my life's work. No way can I put my career on a back burner to baby-sit some mutt."

Melissa tuned him out. She was not at all sure she could handle Savannah's giant Doberman, much less conceal him in a crowded theatre camp. But one thing was certain: The quiet girl owed a lot to Griffin Bing. She'd been a complete loner before he'd recruited her as an electronics expert on one of his operations. She might never have made any friends without him.

If The Man With The Plan thought this was necessary, that was enough for Melissa.

From: Melissa
To: Griffin
Where do we pick up the package?

Twenty-five miles to the west, at Camp Ebony Lake, a smiling Griffin texted a response to Melissa.

From: Griffin
To: Melissa
Don't worry. We deliver.

He put down his phone and set his mind to the details of Operation Hideout: Phase Two.

The plan was dead. Long live the plan.

THE SECOND HIDEOUT

16

The small screen showed the two-lane road cutting a ribbon through the trees as far as the electronic eye could see. Phone in hand, Melissa watched intently.

Logan peered over her shoulder. "Don't tell me you hacked into a satellite."

Melissa agitated her head, creating gaps in the curtain of hair that usually obscured her face. "Of course not. I've just placed a few wireless webcams in the trees." She tapped the screen, and the angle changed slightly.

Logan yawned hugely. "It's too early. How come these plans can't happen at a decent hour? An actor needs plenty of rest to practice his craft to the best of his ability."

Melissa was patient. "The pantry truck doesn't make its run on our schedule. It delivers to all the camps up here at the crack of dawn so everything is ready before the kids get up."

"I'm not feeling my character," Logan warned.

"You don't have to win an Oscar," Melissa soothed. "You just have to get the driver to stop." She tensed. "Get ready. Half a mile."

Sure enough, the white panel truck had appeared in the distance on the monitor.

"All right, I'll do it," Logan conceded. "But it won't be art."

Melissa stepped back into the cover of the trees. "Break a leg," she whispered.

Logan stood a little taller. It was the standard good-luck message for an actor about to take the stage.

He could see the vehicle now, and hear its motor shifting into second gear as it climbed the grade. Logan waited until it was about a hundred yards away, and then stepped out into the road, waving his arms, the picture of confusion.

The truck jerked to a sudden halt, and the driver jumped out. "What's the matter, kid? Are you okay?"

It was just the cue line Logan had been waiting for. "I—I'm not sure." He stared at the man blankly. "What am I doing here? I was in bed a minute ago, and—I must have been sleepwalking!"

The man looked shaken. "It's a good thing I was paying attention. I could have run you down. Can I get you a bottle of water? I've got some in the back—"

"No!" Logan exclaimed, a little too sharply.

If the driver had turned around at that instant, he would have seen Melissa helping Griffin, Savannah, and Luthor out the rear of the payload. It was terrible acting, but it kept the man's attention on Logan instead of the great escape that was taking place behind him.

"What I mean is—" Logan stammered, recovering— "I'm fine now. I'm sorry for stopping you." Luthor and the three kids were almost in the cover of the trees. "You can go."

No sooner were the words out of his mouth than Griffin tripped on a rut and went sprawling headfirst.

"On second thought, I'm feeling woozy again!" Logan fairly bellowed. *No actor should have to work under these conditions. Johnny Depp would never put up with it.*

Logan watched, wide-eyed, as the girls dragged Griffin out of sight, Luthor trotting by their side. Was that a Care Bears shirt Griffin was wearing? Who was in charge of wardrobe for this operation? Not anybody with the right to call himself The Man With The Plan.

"Whoops, false alarm," Logan announced as soon as the others were out of sight.

"Get in the truck," the man offered. "Let me give you a ride home. Are you from that theatre camp?"

Logan's actor's preparation had not included that question. "Of course—" he stammered—"not." The last thing they needed was a concerned truck driver asking questions about a kid wandering out on the road at six o'clock in the morning. "Bye!"

He ran off into the woods, leaving the man scratching his head.

When Logan rejoined the team at a small clearing in the cover of the woods, he found Savannah speaking to Luthor in the quiet manner that had earned her the reputation as Cedarville's premier dog whisperer.

"I have to go back to camp now, sweetie. You'll be staying here with Melissa and Logan. I know it isn't what you had in mind, but you three are going to have so much fun together. . . ."

"Not *too* much fun," Griffin put in. "He has to be quiet. All that barking nearly blew our cover at Ebony Lake."

"And don't forget to tell him about the *serious* theatre going on," Logan added. "This isn't just a camp-camp, it's a *drama* camp, and some of the people here are going to be actors for their real careers. He can't expect us to drop everything and go get dog biscuits or whatever."

Savannah was annoyed. "I won't tell him that. It's insulting. Besides, he wouldn't know what to make of a message like that. An animal's comprehension comes from emotional intelligence and sensitivity."

"He wasn't so sensitive when he was trashing my basement," Logan complained.

Savannah faced him furiously. "If you've got a problem—"

Griffin quickly interposed himself between his two friends. "It works against the plan if we fight among ourselves. The whole point of all this is to keep

Luthor out of Swindle's grubby hands. We're doing you a favor, Savannah."

The dog whisperer was instantly contrite. If it weren't for Operation Hideout, her beloved Doberman would be back with his former owner, the sleazy S. Wendell Palomino.

"Sorry, Logan," she said emotionally. "I'm so grateful to you guys for stashing Luthor up here. It's just not safe for us to keep him at Ebony Lake anymore."

"It helps us, too," Melissa assured her. "If we let Swindle get rich off Luthor's dog show winnings, he'll use the money to come after all of us."

"Keep your eyes peeled for anybody who might be a private investigator working for Swindle," Griffin instructed. "Whoever it is will be undercover, so you have to be careful. Watch out for delivery guys or forest rangers who poke around asking nosy questions. It could even be a new counselor—nobody's above suspicion. Got it?"

Melissa held up her phone for the others to see. "Here comes the laundry truck heading west."

"That's our ride home," Griffin confirmed. He turned to Logan. "Ready for some more acting?"

"The sleepwalking thing isn't really working for me," Logan mused. "You know, dramatically. Maybe I should be a parachutist who blew off course."

"Except there's no parachute," Melissa pointed out.

Logan sighed. "We need a props department."

"Just be something," Griffin hissed. "If we miss the truck, it's a twenty-five-mile hike back to camp."

"Leave Luthor with me," Melissa said courageously. "Go catch your ride."

There wasn't even time for an emotional farewell scene between Savannah and the Doberman. Instead, the animal expert made an elaborate show of handing the leash over to Melissa. "Be a good boy, sweetie. I'll see you soon."

They heard the brakes of the truck, followed by Logan's voice. The young actor had abandoned his parachutist story, and was portraying a lost hiker. There was no time to lose. In another moment, the opportunity would be lost forever.

"Go!" whispered Melissa.

With a brave smile for Luthor's sake, Savannah allowed herself to be pulled away by Griffin. As Logan distracted the driver of the van, the two renegade campers circled around the back of the truck, eased open the rear gate, and hid themselves behind stacks of linens.

The instant Savannah was out of sight, the change in Luthor was glaringly obvious. His calm deserted him, and he began to pace the clearing, twitching nervously.

Shy Melissa Dukakis had only just reached the point where she felt comfortable talking to people. To deal with this very large, very frightening animal was going to take every milligram of fortitude she could muster.

"Calm down—uh—sweetie," she ventured in her best impersonation of Savannah.

The endearment, coming from anybody but his beloved dog whisperer, was not to be tolerated. The growl seemed to begin at the tip of his tail, traveling through that oversized body, and emerging from behind those very sharp teeth.

Melissa nearly swallowed her tongue. "Luthor— uh—sir—" Her hand visibly shaking, she reached into the bag of food Savannah had brought along, and produced a bone-shaped dog treat.

Luthor snapped it down in a flash, but it failed to settle him.

Logan reentered the clearing. "Well, that's done—"

The big dog turned on him with a sharp bark, freezing him on the spot.

Melissa might have been quiet and timid, but her experience with Griffin and his team had taught her one important truth: *Never* let a plan get out of control.

She activated the Skype app on her phone and called Griffin. A shadowy face surrounded by sheets and towels appeared almost immediately. "Are you crazy?" Griffin rasped. "You know we're hiding in the back of a van! You want to get us caught?"

Melissa's wide eyes were clearly visible behind her curtain of hair. "Savannah has to talk to her dog!"

Griffin understood her instantly. Just seconds

later, Savannah appeared on the screen, in full dog-whispering mode. Melissa held the phone up for Luthor to see.

The Doberman was a little bewildered by the tiny Savannah who was here and yet not here. But there was no question—that was her face, and that was her voice, which meant he wasn't so abandoned after all.

Melissa and Logan exchanged a look of pure dismay. Luthor was calm again—but for how long? Would his hostility return the minute Savannah's familiar face was no longer before him?

"Great," Logan said with a nervous laugh. "Now all we have to do is keep her on the phone forever."

Melissa retreated behind her hair. It was going to be a really long three weeks.

17

The buildings of Camp Ta-da! were laid out around its performance center—an old barn converted into a small theater and rehearsal space. It was a tight squeeze to get one hundred fifty campers plus their counselors inside at the same time. But when it was raining—like it was on that day—no one minded the crowding. All eyes were on head counselor and creative director Wendy Demerest, who was running through the details of the annual "Showdown" against the camp's cross-county rivals, Camp Spotlight.

"For the next week we work around the clock to script, stage, and rehearse a forty-five-minute revue," she explained. "At the Showdown, both camps put on dueling shows for a trophy and bragging rights. Spotlight has beaten us the last three summers"—a loud chorus of boos greeted this statement—"and that's why this is the year we bring the cup back to Ta-da!, where it belongs."

Melissa was amazed at the wild cheering that

greeted this announcement. Even Logan—who normally looked at his acting as serious business—was on his feet, punching the air and howling. She had only agreed to go away for the summer because her parents thought she spent too much time alone with her computers. She'd signed on with Logan and Ta-da! in order to avoid all the sports, competition, and rah-rah-rah. Yet here she was in the middle of what looked like a pep rally. It turned out that these drama types were just as crazed over their specialty as the kids at the baseball camp up the road. Rah-rah-rah couldn't be avoided.

As the ovation died down, a distinct *woof* could be heard over the general din. Melissa reached out and pinched Logan's arm, but the campers who *didn't* know there was a dog in the attic hadn't noticed the extra sound.

There had been only one place to hide Luthor, chosen after an intensive search for something safer. Every other building, cabin, Quonset hut, or tent in camp was used regularly. But the hayloft above the rehearsal hall was strictly an off-season storage area. Now that camp was in session, all the props, sets, and costumes had been moved downstairs. The attic was empty, and would remain so until the buses arrived to take the campers home.

There was a thump from upstairs. Unlike the woof, *everyone* heard that. To Melissa it sounded exactly like a large Doberman bumping into a crossbeam.

An uneasy murmur rippled through the campers, but Wendy smiled. "Any theater worth its salt is haunted. Maybe that's our ghost up there—the spirit of some old actor who wants us to beat the pants off Spotlight on the seventeenth. It's good luck."

Everyone laughed, and there was scattered applause.

"Now," Wendy went on, "the title of our revue is *The Best of Broadway*. The first thing we need is a captain for our Camp Ta-da! team. Vote carefully, because our captain will be your leader through every stage of the competition—from scripting to costumes and set design to rehearsals to performance. The nominees are Dante Bryant, Mary Catherine Klinger, and Logan Kellerman."

As the counselors circulated with slips of paper to serve as ballots, Logan flashed Melissa a knowing smile. "It's in the bag," he said confidently. "Everyone knows I'm the best actor in camp. They've probably seen the Vicks commercial I starred in. Nobody does post-nasal drip like a Kellerman!"

In the crush of the crowded theater, a tall counselor accidentally brushed against a hanging cable. As he reached up to steady it, his thumb depressed the operating button. An electrical hum filled the barn, and a rectangular platform began to descend from the ceiling.

Melissa and Logan stared in horror. They'd thought that the only way to get to the attic was via the steep, ladderlike staircase leading from the back of the barn.

They'd had no idea this hoist platform even existed. And there was a pretty good chance that when this thing came down to eye level, Luthor was going to be perched on it!

Shoving campers out of his way, Logan made a screaming run for the descending platform. He got his hands on it and vaulted aboard, prepared to shield the dog from view with his very body. An "oof" escaped him as he landed face-first on the hard metal.

Since all eyes were on Logan's antics, only Melissa noticed the big Doberman head peering down from the opening in the ceiling. Urgently, she waved him back, and was surprised when he obeyed and vanished from view.

The counselor pressed the button again, and the platform was ascending, bearing Logan with it.

"Hey, you guys!" Logan shouted. "Let me down!"

With a click, he was closed into the attic. He reappeared several minutes later after climbing down the ladder. By this time the vote was over. Mary Catherine Klinger was the captain of Ta-da!'s Showdown team.

"*I* voted for you," Melissa consoled Logan.

"One vote!" Logan mourned. "I didn't even get to vote for myself. Mary Catherine the Klingon couldn't act her way out of a wet paper bag! There's no way she could do post-nasal drip like me! She couldn't work up a decent sniffle!"

Melissa resettled her hair so that Logan could see the sincerity in her eyes. "At least Luthor didn't get caught. That's the important thing."

Logan was furious. "The stupid dog hasn't even been here a day yet, and already he's cost me an important stepping-stone in my career. He'd better not cost us the Showdown!"

Melissa didn't make friends easily.

Actually, she didn't make friends at all except where Griffin's plans were involved. It wasn't that she didn't want to be more social; she just never knew what to say to anyone. To the other girls, it was so natural—they stayed up for hours after lights-out, giggling and snacking on cookies they'd stashed away from dinner. Funny—Melissa could hack into top secret data storage facilities or bounce an e-mail off so many servers around the world as to make it virtually untraceable. Yet the natural ease of her bunkmates, whispering, laughing, and chowing down, might as well have been a code with uncrackable protocols. To Melissa, it just didn't compute.

Mary Catherine Klinger was in the next bunk. "Watch out for that Kellerman kid," she warned in a confidential tone. "He's all sour grapes that no one voted for him to be captain. I think he might try to sabotage our production for the Showdown."

Shy as she was, Melissa couldn't let that go unchallenged. She had to speak up for her friend. "Logan would never do anything like that. Theatre is his life's work."

Mary Catherine and the girls looked around, trying

to identify the source of the quiet yet strident words. For some reason, no one noticed Melissa, who was now sitting up in bed.

Mary Catherine got a bead on her at last. "Well, that's what he *says*. I've seen his type before. He acts like super actor, gets everybody to buy into his big pie-in-the-sky ideas. But when it's time to deliver, he'll flake out and leave us with nothing."

"You don't know Logan," Melissa defended him. "He's really talented."

Mary Catherine had a broad, toothy stage smile — the kind that could be seen from the very last row of the balcony. Now her grin abruptly disappeared as she frowned at this new girl. They had been living together in this cabin for a week now. Was it possible that the Ta-da! captain simply hadn't noticed her?

"I don't think I know your name," Mary Catherine said.

"M-Melissa —"

"And what's your specialty, Melissa?" Mary Catherine persisted. "You know, acting, dancing, singing . . . ?"

"I'm good with computers," Melissa offered lamely.

"Computers?" echoed Athena Sizemore, who was never far from Mary Catherine's side. "Then what are you doing at a drama camp?"

Melissa didn't like the direction this discussion was taking. But now that she was in it, she couldn't just quit, could she? Were you allowed to resign from a conversation like it was a chess match? These were the things that came naturally to most people that Melissa just didn't get.

"Well"—she was back behind her hair again, but it wasn't doing her any good. She could feel the other girls' eyes burning into her like lasers—"my parents want me to be more outgoing."

"Nothing brings you out of your shell like singing," Mary Catherine enthused. "And I know a solo in the Showdown that's just *perfect* for you!"

"A solo?" Melissa was horrified. "I can't sing!"

"That's what rehearsal's for," the Ta-da! captain assured her. "We start tomorrow!"

Great, Melissa thought miserably. Now the loudest, pushiest girl in the whole camp had set her sights on turning her into a singer.

That's what I get for sticking up for Logan. . . .

Life was simpler back before she'd had friends. Lonelier, but simpler.

18

It was after midnight by the time all the girls were asleep. Melissa took stock of the steady breathing of her cabinmates, paying special attention to Desiree, the counselor, who was snoring softly. The coast was clear.

Careful not to make a sound, she crept out of the cabin. Sneaking around in the dead of night definitely scared her, but not as much as it used to. If you wanted to be in on Griffin's plans, sneaking was a must-have skill.

Logan was already at the meeting place—hidden behind the low fence that extended from the side door of the performance center. He turned on his flashlight, the beam momentarily blinding her. "What took you so long?" he hissed. "I've been waiting forever!"

"The other girls wouldn't go to sleep," she explained. "Mary Catherine wants me to do a solo in the Showdown. I don't know how to sing!"

Logan was bitter. "I can't get elected team captain

when I'm a professional actor, but you get your own solo!"

"I don't want a solo!" Melissa exclaimed, showing as much temper as Logan had ever seen from her. "Mary Catherine's going to *make* me do one!"

Logan couldn't see past the fact that Mary Catherine was running things and he wasn't. "Who puts a Klingon in charge of a drama team? This place is just like the Golden Globes — it's all fixed."

Melissa reached into her pocket and pulled out a napkin that concealed three salami slices and a half-crushed cupcake. "It was all I could save from dinner. What did you bring?"

Logan looked bewildered. "I'm not hungry."

"Not for you," Melissa explained patiently. "For Luthor."

He shrugged. "It's not *my* dog."

"That's the whole point. Neither of us is Savannah, so we have to bribe him if we expect him to do what we want. If he won't go for a walk, it's going to get messy up there."

They took the stairs up to the loft. When they got to the top, they were greeted by an unfriendly growl . . . and a large white Doberman.

"Hey," Logan whispered. "Did somebody switch dogs on us?"

Melissa trained her flashlight on the ghostly creature before them. It was the real Luthor, all right, covered in the white fluffy stuffing that had once been inside the sleeping bag they'd laid down for his comfort. Savannah's "sweetie" had passed the hours by tearing it to pieces. The big Doberman had also made a mess of the blankets and comforters they'd strewn across the floor to muffle the sound of dog toenails.

Logan took a step back from the ferocious glare he was receiving. "Give him the food — quick."

It was gone in a millionth of a second, and Luthor was advancing on them menacingly.

Melissa had been prepared for this possibility. She had learned from Griffin that a good plan allows for all contingencies. Her phone was already set to the Skype app, and the call was going through to Savannah.

It was so dark under the covers that the girl was barely visible. "Have you lost your minds? It's the middle of the night? I'm surrounded by sleeping girls!"

Melissa did not mince words. "Talk to Luthor!" She held the device in front of the big dog's angry dark eyes.

The change in the Doberman was instant and total. His raised hackles suddenly lay flat as if by magic, and his growl became a delicate whimper. He sat obediently before the screen, drinking in the beloved face and listening to the beloved voice.

"Oh, Luthor, I've been so worried about you. . . ."

"Worry about *us*," Logan put in dramatically. "We're the ones who are about to be ripped to shreds."

"Tell him he needs to go for a walk," Melissa instructed urgently.

Savannah soothed Luthor as Melissa clipped the leash on to his collar. The Doberman balked, however, when they tried to lead him back to the ladderlike steps.

"It's too steep," Savannah explained. "He can go up that kind of staircase, but down scares him. He thinks he'll fall."

In the end, they had to lower Luthor and themselves via the electric hoist platform, praying that no one would notice the power humming in the otherwise silent woods.

At that point, Savannah's Ebony Lake counselor came to investigate the mumbling, so the dog whisperer had to hang up and pretend to be talking in her sleep. Luckily, though, Luthor was so excited at the prospect of escaping his imprisonment in the attic that he bounded out of the barn, dragging Melissa at the end of the leash. Logan stayed behind to raise the platform before scrambling to catch up.

They watched the Doberman run and play in the moonlight, awestruck by his raw boundless energy. Luthor raced around the quadrangle at Thoroughbred speed, as if circling some imaginary triple-crown track. If any bleary-eyed camper happened to stagger out of one of the cabins, the poor kid would be flattened.

"Too bad the Klingon can't see this," Logan said wanly. "Nobody messes with you when you've got a killer dog on your side."

"He's not on our side," Melissa reminded him

nervously. "He's on Savannah's, and she can't stay on Skype for three weeks straight. We're going to have to learn to handle him."

"I'm an actor, not a lion tamer."

"You think *I* am?" It was the closest Melissa ever came to a challenging tone. "I'd rather take on the world's most complicated computer virus."

Luthor leaped to snap at a low-flying moth, sailing four feet off the ground.

"Maybe we should try to reach Savannah again," Logan put in uneasily.

The Doberman continued to frolic in the compound, his breakneck speed slackening as he burned off the pent-up energy of his confinement. Eventually, he trotted over and rejoined them. He wasn't friendly, exactly. But he allowed Melissa to clip the leash back on to his collar. It was time to go for a walk.

For secrecy's sake, they sought the cover of the woods. Logan mumbled uneasily as they strolled, rehearsing lines from the many commercials he'd auditioned for:

". . . the cereal guaranteed to stay crunchy in milk . . . clinically proven to kill bad breath germs on contact . . . does your taco sauce give you heartburn? . . ."

Luthor stopped in his tracks so suddenly that Melissa rear-ended him.

Logan was surprised. "What—?"

Then they spotted the flashlight beam, creating the illusion of moving shadows in the dense foliage.

"The counselors?" Logan whispered fearfully.

"Shhh!" Melissa hissed.

The two campers hunkered down beside the dog and watched as the newcomer approached them. They could just make out his face in the glow of his own flashlight — a man, probably a little past middle age, with a neatly trimmed beard and mustache. *Not a counselor, for sure*, Melissa thought.

As the man grew close, she dared to reach out a hand and cover Luthor's snout, hoping the Doberman would take the hint and stay silent — instead of swallowing her arm halfway to the elbow. Some part of Luthor's show-dog training must have kicked in, because he froze and made no sound.

The man passed no more than ten feet from their hiding place and continued in the direction of the camp. No one spoke until the rustling of his footsteps faded out.

"Who's that?" Logan breathed.

"I don't know, but I don't like it," Melissa replied. "Let's see if we can find out what he's up to."

"Are you crazy?" Logan rasped. "We're out way past curfew with a fugitive dog! If we get caught, we'll be kicked out of the Showdown, and then the Klingon will take over the whole enterprise!"

"Griffin told us to watch out for suspicious strangers," she reminded him. "This guy could be working for Swindle. If they tracked Luthor to Ebony Lake, because of Savannah and Griffin, they could probably find us. Swindle knows all the kids on the team."

They followed the bearded man by the glow of his flashlight. He went all the way to Camp Ta-da!, crossing the compound as if certain of his destination.

Melissa, Logan, and Luthor held up at the edge of the clearing. To Melissa's amazement, the man headed straight for the performance center.

"Did someone tip him off about Luthor and where we're hiding him?" Logan managed, shocked.

"I don't see how. . . ." Yet the evidence was right there in front of them—the stranger striding purposefully toward the converted barn. She turned to Logan. "You raised the platform, right?"

"Of course," Logan replied. "But if he knows where to look . . ."

In trepidation, they listened for the hum of the lift coming down. Nothing.

"Maybe he took the stairs," Melissa whispered.

But a moment later, the flashlight beam reappeared, and the stranger left the barn. Melissa, Logan, and Luthor scrambled to get out of his path, watching as he reentered the woods and moved off in the direction he'd come from. After a few minutes, his footsteps could no longer be heard. Eventually, the light vanished as well.

Melissa was white as a sheet. "Griffin was right! Swindle sent a new spy!"

"Now we have to find another hiding place for Luthor," Logan mourned. "I haven't got that kind of time, you know. It's going to be hard enough to put together a decent show with the Klingon bossing everybody around."

"It seems to me that the safest place in camp is the spot where the guy just looked," Melissa argued. "Now that he's ruled it out, he'll search somewhere else next time."

"That doesn't mean we can relax," Logan argued. "He could be back."

She nodded. "In fact, I think we can count on it."

19

The afternoon was hot — but not half as hot as it was inside the warthog costume. It was raining lightly, and every drop made the fur wet and heavy. The effort required to raise his arm was almost more than Logan could muster.

"Mary Catherine —"

The captain of the Showdown team didn't hear him. She bustled about, barking orders as she assembled her cast for the next number — "Hakuna Matata," from *The Lion King.*

"Mary Catherine!" Logan shouted to project his voice beyond the cocoon.

She peered in his eye-holes. "Yes, Logan?"

"Well . . ." How could he explain it? Here he was, a professional actor, who had been in real TV commercials. And how had she cast him? In an outfit where no one could see if he was acting or not, portraying a neckless swine. "It's just that — well, *anybody* could play this part."

"I know you'll rock it."

"But I don't want to rock a warthog!" he wailed. "I want to play a meaty character!"

She lowered her eyes to the warthog's big stomach. "No one's meatier than Pumbaa."

"Not that kind of meaty! I want multiple dimensions, complicated emotions, inner pain!"

"Pumbaa has lots of inner pain," she reasoned. "He has gas!"

She moved on to Bobby Delancey, who played Timon, leaving Logan seething and sweating. The Klingon was doing this on purpose. She knew that if Wendy saw him acting in a halfway decent role, she'd kick Mary Catherine out and make *him* captain of the Showdown team!

They were all in their places when there was a thunderclap, and pelting rain had them scrambling for cover. By the time Logan lurched into the performance center, the warthog suit had soaked up at least twenty extra pounds of water.

Mary Catherine looked down her nose at him. "Logan, you're going to have to take better care of your costume than that. If it's ruined, your parents get charged, you know."

Logan was too exhausted to argue with her. "Let's just do the number and get it over with."

"This stage is too small for 'Hakuna Matata,'" she decided. "Take off your head, and we'll work on Melissa's solo."

Even through the dense wet fur, Logan heard the whimpered protest from his shy friend.

"I've picked the perfect song," Mary Catherine went on. "'Memory' from the musical *Cats*. It's one of the most famous songs in the history of Broadway, so the audience will be expecting great things."

"I can't—" Melissa stammered. "I mean I don't—I mean I never—"

"This is your part," Mary Catherine said firmly.

Something snapped inside Logan and he threw off the top half of his costume. It would have been very dramatic if he could have tossed it clear in a single swashbuckling motion instead of tunneling out like an escaping prisoner, but true actors had to be able to improvise.

"You don't want her to sing 'Memory' in the Showdown," he accused the Ta-da! captain. "You want her to sing it *here* so you can make fun of her, and then cut her from the performance."

Mary Catherine skewered him with laser eyes. "Well, she can't just do *nothing*. It's a group revue. Everyone's supposed to take part. Those are the rules, you know."

"I can work on set design," Melissa offered.

At that moment, a loud yelp resounded directly above them.

"The performance center ghost!" exclaimed Athena with an anxious laugh.

"No, that's not it," Logan put in quickly. "A falling branch must have hit the roof."

The campers regarded one another nervously. None of them had ever heard a tree branch bark before.

The Showdown was always held outdoors. The stage was at the base of a large hill, which served as a natural grandstand for the audience. Each year the host camp was in charge of building a set and a lighting arc on the existing platform.

Dozens of upturned eyes watched in amazement as the chandelier rolled over the top of the array and came hurtling down to the stage. A crash of shattering glass blasted from the speakers.

The campers all gasped—and then applauded. Hunched behind her laptop on a tree stump, Melissa took a small bow. Behind her hair, her face flushed as it always did when she received any kind of attention.

"Wow!" Logan exclaimed, goggle-eyed. He'd always known his friend was a genius, but he'd never imagined that her tech skills could be applied to the theatre!

"Not bad." Mary Catherine didn't look too pleased at the idea of credit going to anyone except herself. But this special effect—for their *Phantom of the Opera* number—couldn't be ignored. "Definitely pretty good."

Melissa pounded the keyboard and the "chandelier" rose on its system of ropes and pulleys and disappeared behind the arc lights, poised for its next fall.

"How did you make it *sound* so real?" asked Athena breathlessly. "I mean, the chandelier's just a wooden scenery board! I could have sworn it was glass breaking into a million pieces!"

"I downloaded the clip from the Internet," Melissa replied in a voice so soft that everyone had to strain to hear. "I also got jungle sounds for *The Lion King*, a helicopter rotor for *Miss Saigon*, and a tornado for *The Wizard of Oz*."

During break time, Logan and Melissa walked along Ta-da!'s "Main Street," which featured the mess hall, pool, and camp offices.

"The Klingon gave me my part for the Charlie Brown skit," Logan said savagely. "I'm Snoopy."

"What's wrong with that?" asked Melissa. "Snoopy's one of the main characters."

"No lines!" Logan complained. "I don't even bark. I just crawl around on my hands and knees wearing aviator's goggles. First the warthog and now this. What's next? *Mary Poppins*? I can play the umbrella."

So wrapped up was he in his complaints that he failed to notice the bearded man chatting with Wendy Demerest.

"Look!" Melissa took Logan's wrist and pulled him around the corner of the wash station. "It's that guy—the one we saw in the woods! Swindle's spy."

Logan peered around the building, frowning. "If he's a spy, how come he knows Wendy?"

Melissa was not fooled. "Remember what Griffin

told us about Malachi Moore? The first thing he did was make friends with all the counselors at Ebony Lake."

"Did he have a beard?" Logan whispered.

"There are a dozen fake beards in the wardrobe cabin," she pointed out. "But I don't think this is the same person. Griffin said Malachi was young. This guy's older than my dad."

Another counselor joined Wendy and the stranger, and soon the group was laughing over a joke the two campers could not make out.

"What can we do?" asked Logan. "Walk up and accuse him of being a dognapper? What if somebody asks us how we know? The last thing we want is for the counselors to find out about Luthor."

"Good point." Melissa frowned. What would Griffin do? *There's always a plan,* he was fond of saying. *If you look hard enough, you'll see it.*

"Well, if we can't prove he's working for Swindle," she mused, "maybe we can put him off Luthor's scent."

"How are we supposed to do that?"

"It's not going to be easy," she admitted. "It'll take skill—*acting* skill."

Logan was instantly on board.

20

The fish came from out of nowhere, catching the man full in the face across his short-clipped beard.

"What the—?" He staggered back, stunned, staring at the boy in the Camp Ta-da! T-shirt who stood like a sentry, a ten-inch perch dangling from the end of his rod and reel.

"Sorry, mister." Logan was in character, the picture of apology. "I didn't mean to hurt you."

The victim rubbed his jaw. "What's with the fish around here? Are they made of cement?"

The blush in Logan's cheeks was not acting. He and Melissa could not have ensured that they'd catch a fish from the camp pond. So they had borrowed one from the freezer in the kitchen. It wasn't Logan's fault that there had been insufficient time to thaw it out before it had to be used. Some things in theatre couldn't be scripted in advance. "The northern perch is known for being solid."

The man didn't seem too angry. "I thought this camp was for actors, not anglers."

"We're all actors, but they let us do other things in our spare time," Logan explained, launching into the character he had carefully prepared. "I like to fish because my father's a fish and game expert for the federal government. My name is Ferris Atwater, Jr." It was Logan's favorite alias. "I'm not really a camper here. I just come during the day while my dad's working in the area. He has to catch a feral dog."

"A what?"

"A feral dog is a pet dog that gets lost and starts to live in the wild," Logan supplied. "Dad suspects this one used to be a guard dog, because he's a big Doberman, and kind of mean. The fish and game department thinks he might be dangerous to other wildlife, and even people."

The plan was to convince Swindle's spy that Luthor wasn't being hidden in the camp somewhere, but was out in the woods, running free.

The man must have been almost as good an actor as Logan, because he appeared completely disinterested. "Yeah, well, watch where you're waving that fishing rod, Ferris. The hook could take someone's eye out."

"I'll be careful, Mr. — uh — I'm sorry, I didn't catch your name."

"Smith," the man said quickly. "E. J. Smith."

Logan held out his hand. "Good to meet you, Mr. Smith. Do you live around here?"

"I have a summer place up on the mountain." Mr. Smith pulled back from Logan's grip. "Your hand is like ice!"

Uh-oh. "It's the bait," Logan exclaimed glibly. "My worms were in the fridge." That was a close one! "Anyway, good meeting you." He pulled a phone from the pocket of his shorts and snapped a picture.

The bearded man was suddenly angry. "What did you do that for?"

"In case the feral dog gets you," Logan explained reasonably. "My dad needs to know everyone who's in harm's way."

"I can look after myself!" growled E. J. Smith. "You delete that!"

"Okay, sure." Following Melissa's instructions, Logan carefully saved the photograph before erasing it from the screen.

"I don't like pictures," the man said gruffly. "I come up here for privacy, not to end up on some fish and game website!" He stormed off, giving the swinging perch a wide berth.

A smile found its way to Logan's lips. Maybe Mary Catherine didn't appreciate his talent, but there was more than one way for an actor to practice his craft.

This had been another successful performance.

* * *

Griffin's face filled the small screen of Melissa's phone as he examined the photograph of E. J. Smith. "No, it's definitely not Malachi," he concluded. "But Swindle could've hired another goon."

It was after midnight, and Melissa and Logan were in the attic of the performance center, bringing Luthor his dinner. Across the hayloft, the Doberman was diving into seven feet of link sausages filched from the freezer on the same raid as the one that had netted the northern perch. It was a special treat for the dog, who had been surviving on table scraps and whatever could be smuggled to him in pockets and under hoodies.

"That's what we figured," Melissa agreed in a low voice. "I googled him, and it turns out E. J. Smith was the captain of the *Titanic*. So this guy's definitely using an alias."

"Never mind that." Savannah bumped Griffin out of the frame. "How close do you think he is to finding Luthor?"

"He hasn't got a clue," Logan assured her. "My performance was legendary. He's probably out in the woods right now, searching for a feral dog by flashlight."

"My poor sweetie." Savannah sighed in relief.

It was the one word that could have dislodged Luthor from the sausages. Up perked his ears, and he scrambled over to Savannah's image on the phone.

"Oh, Luthor, I miss you so much! Are you being a good boy?"

In answer, a mammoth tongue came out and slurped across the small screen.

Melissa was horrified. "Moisture is not good for electronics!" She wiped the device on her pajama bottoms.

Griffin brought them back to the original point of the call. "Well, it isn't Malachi, but the new goon's definitely dirty. He even looks kind of familiar, but I can't place him."

"I thought so, too," put in Melissa. "Could he be from Cedarville?"

"I doubt it," Griffin replied. "Swindle would never hire someone we might recognize. Anyway, it seems like you've got this guy under control — for now. But be careful. If he keeps nosing around, you're going to have to find out more about him."

21

The union soldiers stood on the stage—a line of blue uniforms behind the grave markers of Gettysburg National Cemetery. They saw the tall stovepipe hat first, followed by the famous beard. And then he was before them—Abraham Lincoln, sixteenth president of the United States.

The president glanced at his notes on the back of an envelope, and launched into Lincoln's famous speech. "Four score and seven years ago . . ."

A soldier broke ranks and pointed a finger at the president. "This isn't right at all!"

Lincoln—played by Bobby Delancey—looked first at his accuser and then at Mary Catherine. "That's not in the script!"

Logan threw off his hat, nearly removing his nose with the chinstrap. "When Lincoln delivered the Gettysburg address, he was coming down with smallpox! Where's your rash?"

Bobby was bewildered. "Nobody said I had to have a rash!"

"A real actor doesn't just learn lines!" Logan couldn't hide his disgust at Bobby's amateurism. "We have to be able to feel the heat from your fever. And your nausea—you haven't even gagged! If we're going to beat Camp Spotlight, we have to go all out!"

Mary Catherine stormed onto the stage. "Logan, get back to your mark. You're a soldier. You have no lines in this scene."

Logan bristled. "That's the whole problem, isn't it? I have no lines in *any* scene. I can do Lincoln like nobody's business. Or Hamlet. Have you ever seen my *Crucible*? Nobody gets burned at the stake better than me! But you've got me playing four-legged creatures and a soldier with a plastic rifle!"

Wendy stepped onto the stage. "There are no stars here; we're actors in a troupe. And all roles, big and small, are equally important. If we fight among ourselves, we're giving Camp Spotlight an advantage over us." When Logan looked stubborn, she added, "It's up to you, Logan. If you can't be satisfied with the parts you've been given, I'm going to have to drop you from the cast."

Her words finally penetrated Logan's resentment. His roles might be insignificant and insulting. But nothing would be worse than being out of the Showdown. That was the reason he'd come to Ta-da! in the first place.

After rehearsal, as he and Melissa headed for the mess hall for lunch, Logan's bitterness spilled over. "This is all Savannah's fault! It's thanks to her that we're saddled with Luthor in the attic of the performance center — which is the only reason *I* didn't get picked to be captain!"

"It's not just about Luthor," Melissa reminded him. "Once Swindle's done with the dog, he's going to come after the rest of us. It's his revenge for the baseball card heist."

They stepped into the wood-framed building and froze in the doorway. There in the lunch line, helping himself to chicken pot pie, was none other than E. J. Smith.

"What's he doing here?" Logan hissed in consternation. "Why isn't he out in the woods looking for the feral dog?"

"Maybe he didn't believe you," Melissa whispered back.

"Are you kidding? I *killed*!"

"You know, Griffin's right," she commented. "He really does look familiar. We've got to find out who he is."

"Well, he definitely isn't who he says he is," added Logan. "E. J. Smith is at the bottom of the Atlantic."

"If only I could get to his computer," Melissa mused. "Then I'd know more about him than his own mother."

"How are you going to that?" asked Logan. "He doesn't carry a laptop with him."

At that moment, Melissa caught her reflection in

the glass sneeze-guard that covered the salad bar. Her expression matched one that she'd often seen on the face of The Man With The Plan. "Remember what he told you: His house is up on the hill somewhere. We can follow him, figure out where he lives. That's where the computer is going to be."

Logan was wide-eyed. "And break in?"

She nodded grimly. "You heard Griffin. We have to find out more about this guy."

From: Melissa
To: Griffin
Followed E. J. Smith yesterday. He lives in cabin not far from camp. Hoping to get on his computer to learn true identity.

From: Griffin
To: Melissa
We'll make a planner of you yet! Good luck!

22

W e're lost."

Logan slumped against a tree, unable to go on.

"We're not lost." Melissa's hair concealed the fact that she was rolling her eyes. "We're going the right way. It's just a little bit farther."

Two days had passed since they'd tailed Swindle's agent back to his summer home. Now, finally, the coast was clear. E. J. Smith was with the Ta-da! campers and counselors in the performance center, watching video of the various musical numbers and dramatic scenes of their revue. It was a little nerve-racking that Luthor was in the attic directly above so many people, including a professional dognapper. An accidental slip of the wrist could send the Doberman on a steady whirring descent into the midst of the entire population of the camp.

It wasn't very long before the path rounded a dense

grove of pines, and there it was, a small cottage of log and stone, nestled against the hillside. It looked exactly like Smith's cover story—a summer residence in the woods, perfect for a city dweller to get away from it all. What it did not resemble was a dognapper's lair. But they knew the truth.

Logan was getting cold feet. "Don't ask me to pick the lock. I'm an actor, not a burglar."

Melissa tried the door, but the knob didn't budge. They examined the windows. All locked.

"If we break a window," Logan reasoned, "he'll know someone's been inside."

Frowning, Melissa raised her head until she found herself looking at a small window in the low A-frame attic. The sash was clearly raised a few inches. "There," she said. "That's the way in."

"If you're a squirrel," said Logan, following her gaze. It was an awfully small window. "A baby squirrel."

"Ben climbs into smaller places than that," Melissa pointed out. In addition to being Griffin's best friend, Ben served as the team's tight-spaces specialist.

"Ben's half the size of me," Logan protested. "He goes in there because he fits!"

"Fair enough." Melissa sighed. "I'll do it. Just give me a boost to the porch roof."

"Oh, right!" snapped Logan. "Leave me standing here for when E. J. Smith comes back!"

At last, Melissa ended the argument by forming

a basket with her interlaced fingers. Logan stepped aboard, and she heaved him upward.

The disaster unfolded quickly. He got his hand onto the roofing shingles, but floundered there, unable to find anything to hold on to. As he wriggled, his free foot kicked Melissa in the mouth. She went down, leaving him unsupported. He tried to hoist his leg onto the roof, but succeeded only in getting it tangled in the chain of a hanging pot. The chain snapped. Down came the pot, and Logan with it, landing hard beside Melissa and the shattered planter. Clay shards and dirt scattered everywhere.

"Look what you've done!" he accused Melissa. "No way can we hide that we've been here now!"

"What *I've* done?" And then she saw it, half-buried in the fallen earth—a well-worn key. "We're in!"

The house was small and neat, with wood-paneled walls and handmade rustic furniture. Over the fireplace hung a painting of E. J. Smith himself, with a velvet jacket and silk Ascot tie. It gave Melissa a moment's unease.

"If he's only here to go after Luthor, why would he bring a picture of himself to hang over the mantel?"

Logan peered into the single small bedroom. "Let's just find the computer and get out. If we get caught, we'll be sent home. And all those hours in a warthog suit will be for nothing."

They found the computer on the kitchen table, and

Melissa wasted no time booting it up. "You know, this is really slow," she commented. "He should defrag his hard drive. And an anti-malware scan wouldn't hurt. Who knows how many viruses he might have?"

"I don't care if he has the black plague," Logan retorted. "That painting is freaking me out! It's like he's watching us ransacking his house."

"It's not my fault he neglects basic computer maintenance," Melissa said crossly. "Okay — I'm opening his e-mail program."

And then a voice from outside the house announced, "Blasted raccoons! Look at the mess!"

Logan froze. "E. J. Smith!" he croaked.

Two pairs of eyes flashed to the front of the house. Through the window, they could see Smith, bending over his broken planter.

A moment later, the doorknob was turning.

"Hide!" It was barely a whisper, but no syllable ever resonated louder. Logan knew that an actor must always be able to think on his feet, because anything could happen in live theatre. But at that moment, the only action that came to him was a frantic dance in the middle of the living room.

The door began to swing wide. In a second, the dognapper would be upon them.

It was Melissa who grabbed him by the arm, hauled him across the living room, stuffed him behind the sofa, and squeezed in after him. She ducked her head out of sight just as the bearded man came into the living room and flopped down on the couch.

"Man, what a scorcher!" By the third breath, he was snoring.

Trapped behind the furniture, Logan motioned that they should make a break for it. Melissa shook her head, and mouthed the words, "Not yet." It was too risky with the dognapper inches away from them.

"But we can't stay here forever!" Logan squeaked.

The sound jarred Smith awake, and he looked around for the source. Then his eyes fell on the computer. "Did I leave that on all day?" He got up and walked into the kitchen.

Melissa and Logan crouched in uncomfortable misery while Smith phoned tech support, and tried to convince the agent that his computer had been on for six hours and hadn't yet gone to screen-saver mode.

Melissa's mind raced. What to do? Ordinarily, she took a lot of guidance from The Man With The Plan. But she couldn't remember Griffin ever being stuck in a spot like this. She tried to troubleshoot the problem logically, as she would a technological glitch. But people were not predictable like computers. Would Smith turn away long enough for them to get out the front door? It was risky, but if they couldn't get out of here, sooner or later, they would be missed back at camp. When would the point come where the consequences of *that* outweighed the danger of being caught here?

Logan shifted his position, and something fell out of his pocket, hitting the floor with a soft thud. It was a large candy caterpillar left over from the last "Hakuna Matata" rehearsal. Timon and Pumbaa had to eat bugs while singing. Yes, it was a stage prop, but at that moment, Logan was grateful for something to snack on. He carefully bisected the gummy creature, and he and Melissa enjoyed an early meal.

The time ticked by with agonizing slowness. After an hour, Logan indicated that he was leaving, no matter what. They had a totally silent screaming match, complete with red faces and arm gestures.

By then, Smith was cooking dinner, and spicy curry fumes were making their eyes water. At last, nearly ninety minutes into the ordeal, a break! E. J. Smith left his creation to simmer on the stove, and stepped into the cottage's small bathroom.

Melissa and Logan did not wait for an engraved invitation. They burst from behind the couch and blasted out the front door, never risking a backward glance. Stiff-legged and cramped, they staggered through the woods and down the mountainside, tripping over exposed roots and getting caught up in low branches.

Back at the cabin, E. J. Smith emerged from the bathroom to a peculiar sight. His sofa was pushed away from the wall, and his front door was ajar. Maybe he'd been absentminded about leaving the computer on, but he'd definitely closed the door. He walked over to the couch, and was about to push it back into place against the wall when he saw it—a gummy candy in the form of a caterpillar. He never ate candy. It was bad for the waistline and the complexion.

The evidence began to add up: the broken planter, the working laptop, the out of place couch, the foreign candy, the open door.

Someone had been in his house.

I've worked here fifteen years, and this summer's revue is the best I've ever seen! Give yourselves a hand, people!"

Wendy's praise brought cheers from the entire population of Camp Ta-da!

"The Showdown is scheduled to begin at three o'clock tomorrow," the head counselor went on. "The buses from Camp Spotlight should arrive around noon. We'll begin with the traditional barbecue lunch, and then we'll start to get into our costumes. As the visitors, Spotlight will go on first. And then we get last licks. The weather forecast is perfect, we've got a great show and a lot of talented performers. This is the year we break the streak—I can feel it in my bones!"

The campers liked the sound of that.

As the ovation died down, one of the junior counselors rushed up onstage and whispered in Wendy's ear. A moment later, Mr. Worling, the camp director, appeared in the company of none other than E. J. Smith.

In the back row, Logan and Melissa held their collective breath.

Mr. Worling stepped forward, his face grave. "I have a serious matter that can't wait. One or more of our campers was where they shouldn't have been yesterday. The woods are off-limits beyond camp property, but this goes deeper than that. This goes to the level of breaking and entering and trespassing on private property."

"Don't worry," Melissa whispered to Logan, who was draining of all color. "He never saw us. There's no way anybody could know who it was."

E. J. Smith joined the camp director. "The culprit left *this* on the floor behind my couch." He held up what looked like a colorful fat shoestring.

All the air came out of Melissa and Logan. It was a gummy caterpillar.

"A piece of candy?" Wendy exclaimed. "That could have come from anybody. Who knows how long it's been there?"

"Oh! *Oh!*" Mary Catherine's hand shot up. "That's one of the caterpillars Timon and Pumbaa eat during 'Hakuna Matata'!"

"Well, it couldn't have been Timon," Wendy reasoned. "Bobby was sitting right next to me for the videos yesterday. Who plays Pumbaa?"

Mary Catherine was on her feet, pointing. "Logan! Logan did it! It was Logan!"

"Don't admit anything!" Melissa hissed. "They have no proof!"

But it would have taken a lot more than that to settle Logan down. A cornered animal will either attack or play dead. Not Logan Kellerman. He could be counted upon to launch into a dramatic scene.

"All right, I did it! And I'm proud! That man is not who he says he is! E. J. Smith went down with the *Titanic* a hundred years ago!"

There was a buzz of confusion. What did the *Titanic* have to do with gummy caterpillars?

"We were protecting the poor man's privacy!" Wendy tried to explain.

But Logan was not to be stopped. "He's no 'poor man'!" he thundered. "He's a ruthless, low-down, slimy dognapper!"

To the crowd, this made even less sense than the *Titanic*. Why would there be a dognapper in the middle of the woods, where there were no dogs?

Wendy's eyes bulged. "What dog?"

Logan opened his mouth to reply, but at that moment, Melissa tackled him to the ground.

Mr. Worling's face was a thundercloud. "Have you all lost your minds? This is no dognapper, and he's certainly not the captain of the *Titanic*! Take a good look at him! He's Mickey Bonaventure, the famous actor, and every year he summers in these woods! And to show the kind of good neighbor he is, he's volunteered to be the judge of the Showdown!"

Melissa squinted at the bearded man. No wonder he was so familiar! Mickey Bonaventure had been a major movie star back in the '80s. His movies were still on TV, if you stayed up after midnight. The person before them was thirty years older now, and the beard covered part of his face. But there was no question that this was the same guy.

The *"Aaaahhh!"* of recognition from the campers soon faded as the pleasant surprise of meeting a celebrity turned sour. Mickey Bonaventure had the power to decide the winner of tomorrow's contest — and Logan had broken into his house and called him a low-down, slimy dognapper. What if that cost them the Showdown? Dozens of angry faces sought out the guilty party, who was lying face-first in the dirt, where Melissa had leveled him.

Logan could feel the hostility roiling around him. All actors, he knew, had to suffer for their art.

But this was ridiculous.

The infirmary was a small white building next to the mess hall. Logan lay on one of the cots, a cold cloth on his forehead and a hot water bottle under his feet. He had taken this treatment upon himself. The nurse had not done anything for him. She was not talking to him, like everyone else in the camp. He had prejudiced the judge against Ta-da!, spoiling their best chance ever to snap the Showdown losing streak. He was not a camper anymore. He wasn't even a human being. He was something to be put out with the trash.

The only person who stuck by him was Melissa. "Maybe it'll be okay," she told him, trying to cheer him up.

He was inconsolable. "Nothing is ever going to be okay again. Mickey Bonaventure! Why didn't I know? I should have felt the aura of a fellow actor!"

"Maybe it was the beard that threw you off," she suggested lamely. "He looks pretty different now."

"He's the only person I've ever met who's got connections in Hollywood! Someone who could have recognized my talent, taken me under his wing, introduced me to the right people! And what did I do? I called him a low-down dognapper!"

"A low-down, *slimy* dognapper," Melissa amended.

"He'll never work with me now!" Logan lamented. "He hates me. I mean, everybody hates me, but I only care about him! He's probably already phoned all the big movie studios and warned them never to hire me!"

"That's okay," Melissa reasoned. "Because he thinks your name is Ferris Atwater, Jr. Logan Kellerman is still clean."

"My life is over."

"It is not," Melissa said stoutly. "You have plenty to

be thankful for. You're not kicked out of camp. You're not even kicked out of the Showdown."

"Only because it's too late to train a new warthog," Logan mourned.

"There's only one thing that bothers me," Melissa mused.

"You're lucky," Logan moaned. "There are about six hundred that bother me."

"Believe it or not, Logan Kellerman, this isn't all about you. Think! If Mickey Bonaventure is innocent, we could still have a dognapper on the loose. And whoever it is has had all the time in the world while we focused on the wrong person."

From: Melissa
To: Griffin
E. J. Smith not dognapper. We blew it.

Over the years, Melissa Dukakis had sent tens of thousands of texts, e-mails, IMs, tweets, and electronic communications of every possible variety. But this one was the hardest by far.

She had let down her friends.

24

CAMP TA-DA! WELCOMES CAMP SPOTLIGHT

The banner stretched between two trees high across the dirt drive that led into Ta-da! Campers lined both sides of the road, cheering and calling greetings as the buses roared into the compound.

Logan could barely raise his head high enough to get a look at the arriving competition. This should have been the greatest day of his life, the day that he'd prove his talent in front of a real Hollywood insider. But now the Showdown was already lost, thanks to him, and he was Public Enemy Number One. How could it be any worse?

Over the excited shouts, he distinctly heard the muffled sound of a dog howling.

His head snapped up, and he looked at Melissa. "Was that what I think it was?"

She nodded gravely. "The counselors were patrolling the compound last night. I couldn't get Luthor any food or take him for his walk."

"He won't starve up there, will he?"

"I checked some online dog sites this morning," Melissa replied. "He's okay for now. The problem is that, the hungrier he gets, the louder he's going to be. And it's only a matter of time until someone figures out where all that howling is coming from."

The buses unloaded, and the host campers greeted the competition and began to escort them toward the main compound, where burgers and hot dogs already sizzled on charcoal grills.

One of the drivers approached the Spotlight head counselor. "Hey, lady, we're done here, right? You don't need us till it's time to leave?"

The woman said something about the drivers being invited for lunch, but Melissa's whirling mind missed all that.

"Logan!" she hissed. "That bus driver—he doesn't know the name of his own boss!"

Logan glared at her. "My career is ruined, and you expect me to care that some total stranger is a little forgetful?"

"Think of the Ta-da! drivers," she persisted. "Most of them have been working here for years. They not only know all the counselors' names, they remember most of ours!"

Logan shrugged. "So the regular driver got sick, and they had to hire a new guy. Happens all the time."

The driver brushed past them, and it was all Melissa and Logan could do to keep from crying out. Folded in the man's shirt pocket was a newspaper clipping they both recognized instantly. Logan had a copy of it taped to his bedroom mirror; Melissa used it as wallpaper for several of her computers and mobile devices. It was an article about the Global Kennel Society Dog Show, and the picture was of Luthor.

"It's him!" Melissa breathed. "The dognapper!"

The fact that the enemy was upon them for real jolted Logan out of his funk. "We've got to keep him from finding out Luthor's here!"

A mournful canine howl wafted on the air.

The man stiffened, trying to pinpoint the direction of the sound. The other driver rushed over, and they held a whispered conference, scanning the various buildings.

"I'll bet *he's* in on it, too," Logan concluded. "Swindle couldn't get Luthor with one dognapper, so he sent two guys this time."

"We have to stop them," Melissa said with determination.

They joined the barbecue, socking away as many

burgers as they ate. Luthor was going to be extra hungry today. But their eyes never left the two bus drivers. On the surface, the men were eating lunch, helping themselves to hot dogs and drinks. But it was obvious that they were scouting out Camp Ta-da!, wandering on the periphery of the party, peering into cabins and other buildings. Every now and then, one of them would drop a napkin and stoop to pick it up, checking the crawl spaces under the structures. And, Melissa noted with a sinking heart, they were working their way closer and closer to the performance center. Sooner or later they'd get to a place where the dog's barking would betray his location in the barn.

"Ferris — can I have a word?"

Logan had been so wrapped up following *today's* dognappers that he hadn't given a thought to *yesterday's*. He turned to find himself staring into the famous features of Mickey Bonaventure.

Face-to-face with the Hollywood connection he'd let slip away, Logan just started babbling uncontrollably. "Mr. Bonaventure, I'm so sorry! I didn't mean to call you slimy! I mean, I meant to call you slimy, but in a good way! Not that it's good to be slimy! And anyway, you're not slimy anymore, not that you ever were—"

The Hollywood star looked impatient. "I've heard a rumor that Camp Ta-da! thinks I'm going to decide against them because of what you did. I want you to know that nothing could be further from the truth."

Logan wanted to pay attention, but the bus drivers

were right outside the barn now. And—was that a bark?

"I take my judging very seriously," Bonaventure went on. "And I intend to be fair and impartial . . . Are you even listening to me?"

"Fer-ris," Melissa prompted meaningfully.

"Not now!" Logan hissed.

The dognappers stepped through the rear door of the performance center, and Melissa broke into a run after them.

"I would never let a personal bias interfere with my responsibilities," the actor droned on. "I'm willing to let bygones be bygones." He held out his hand.

Logan barely noticed it. All his attention was focused on the barn, and the fact that Luthor was trapped there with two dognappers. "I—" he stammered. "I—I gotta go!" He turned his back on his only Hollywood connection and sprinted for the performance center.

He ran into the barn, and was about to burst into the main theater section when he heard soft footsteps creeping up the back staircase. Melissa. And another sound—the growling of a dog. He caught up with his partner on the stairs, and a knowing glance passed between them: Maybe Luthor could take care of himself.

Then a voice from above said, "Hold still, mutt. You won't feel a thing."

Logan remembered Griffin's description of the incident at Ebony Lake. Tranquilizer darts! No one could take on Luthor straight-up. But if the dog was out cold . . .

They blasted up the stairs and arrived in the hayloft to behold a horrible sight. The two bus drivers were trying to corner a nervous Luthor. The younger man with the spiky hair waved a dart gun, struggling to get a bead on the pacing Doberman.

"Get away from our dog!" Logan ordered in his most commanding tone.

"*Your* dog? This dog belongs to a man named Palomino!" growled the older man. "Now get lost! This is none of your business."

Melissa picked up Luthor's water dish and wielded it like a Frisbee.

Spiky Hair laughed. "What are you going to do — knock us out with a plastic bowl?"

In answer, Melissa flung the dish, not at the drivers, but at the upstairs control for the electric lift mechanism.

25

The spinning dish bounced off the wall switch. With a click, followed by a loud hum, the trap door began to descend, lowering the two shocked men down to the theater below. To them, it seemed as if the very floor beneath their feet was falling away. Spiky Hair, struggling to maintain his balance, fired one shot from the tranquilizer gun. The dart nicked Luthor on the neck and sailed beyond him, burying itself in a crossbeam.

Luthor stood, barking through the hole in the floor at his attackers as Melissa and Logan rushed over.

Melissa immediately noticed a red scratch by Luthor's collar. "He's hit!"

"He seems okay to me!" Logan observed, hauling on the leash to urge the Doberman away from the opening, toward the back stairs.

"No, he doesn't!" Melissa exclaimed. "He isn't fighting — he isn't even growling at us! That's not Luthor!"

Sure enough, the big dog's eyes were glazed, his movements slowed.

"Well, I like him better this way!" Logan said feelingly. "Call me crazy, but I've got a thing about having my head bitten off!"

They could hear the lift mechanism still laboring, but knew there wasn't much time before the two drivers hopped down and came around to intercept them. The only way out was the steps. The dog had refused those before, but now he did not balk at the staircase, even though his legs buckled a little. The glancing blow from the dart had delivered some of the dose of the tranquilizer, but not all of it. It did not put him to sleep, yet it was affecting him, making him drowsy and docile.

They reached the bottom of the stairs just in time to see the two drivers charging up the central aisle of the theater toward them. Logan hauled Luthor outside and Melissa slammed the door shut behind them, jamming a fallen tree limb where the bar had once been.

There was a crash from inside, followed by loud pounding. The branch shook but held firm.

"Let's get out of here!" urged Melissa.

"Yeah, but to where?" Logan demanded, breaking into a jog, leading the sluggish dog. "What hiding place could ever be good enough? Once the Showdown starts, we'll be tied up, and those two guys will be free to search the camp one blade of grass at a time!"

"Keep moving!" Melissa panted. He had a point,

but there was no time to think the matter through. Pretty soon, the bus drivers would give up on the back door and exit through the front. When that happened, Luthor had to be *gone*.

Desperately, she looked around. They could try to stash Luthor in the maintenance shed or equipment shack, or stuff him under a bunk in one of the cabins. What was the least likely place the dognappers would check? Would Luthor stay put there? What if one of the counselors walked in on him? It left a lot up to chance.

No, they needed more control. They had to be able to keep an eye on the Doberman every minute. But how?

The barbecue was winding down. Soon it would be time to break into teams for the Showdown, but right now the campers stood in clusters, chatting, joking — anything to suppress preperformance jitters. One of the larger groups included Mary Catherine, Athena, Bobby, and several other key players in the Ta-da! revue. Melissa took the leash from Logan and headed toward them, Luthor stumbling drowsily behind.

"You can't let anybody *see* him!" Logan hissed after her. When he realized her destination, his whisper became even more urgent. "You can't let the *Klingon* see him! She's the enemy!"

She led Luthor right into their midst and gestured urgently for them to form a circle around him. "We have to hide this poor dog!" she begged.

Mary Catherine's eyes bulged. "Are you crazy? There

are no dogs allowed at camp! Where did you get it?"

"He's from one of the farms around here," Melissa explained, inventing rapidly. "And the farmer is *cruel* to him!" Okay, it was a lie. But if the dognappers got hold of Luthor, they'd bring him to Swindle, who'd be every bit as cruel as her imaginary farmer. So there was truth at the core of the fiction.

"Dog abusers, dognappers," Mary Catherine scoffed. "What is it with you two and dogs?"

"We thought Mickey Bonaventure was working for the farmer," Logan put in. "That's why I called him a dognapper. I thought he was after this poor little guy — okay, big guy."

The circle tightened protectively around Luthor. Over her shoulder, Melissa spied the two bus drivers bursting out the front entrance of the performance center. This group of campers was all that stood between the Doberman and capture. Somehow, they had to make it work.

"If we get caught hiding a dog," Mary Catherine argued, "we could be kicked out of camp. Not to mention that it's not our dog, and we have no right to keep it from its rightful owner."

"Have a heart, Mary Catherine," put in Athena. "Look how sad he is. He can barely hold up his head."

"You can tell he's got a mean owner," added Bobby.

"That's not our problem," Mary Catherine insisted. "The Showdown is the most important day of our summer." She sneezed. "And anyway, I'm allergic. We'll turn the dog over to Mr. Worling. He'll know what to do."

Logan spoke up. "We can't do that. We just can't." His voice brimmed with emotion. "You know how adults are. He'll say the dog is property and has to go back to the farmer. I can't live with myself if that happens. A dog is loyal and innocent and trusting. He can't stand up to an abusive owner. He can't defend himself. That's up to people." A short sob escaped him. "That's up to *us*."

Melissa regarded her friend with a new respect. She had seen Logan's acting performances before, but this was different. This was from the heart.

Logan dropped to his knees and hugged Luthor, who was tranquilized just enough to put up with it. "Don't worry, sweetie. We won't let you down."

Melissa adjusted her thinking. Logan was playing a part after all. He was portraying Savannah Drysdale.

"Of course we won't!" Athena declared.

All at once, the other campers in the circle blurted out their support.

"We're with you all the way!"

"We've got your back, dog!"

"That bad farmer's never going to hurt you again!"

Luthor emitted a confused gurgle of appreciation.

"Fine," said Mary Catherine. "What do we have to do?"

Melissa glanced across the compound. The bus drivers had split up, and were investigating the cabins one by one. "If we can keep him safe until after the Showdown, maybe we can get Mr. Worling to call the ASPCA or something." It was another lie, but once the performances were over and the contest had been decided, Swindle's men would no longer have any excuse to hang around searching. They'd have to take the visitors home to Camp Spotlight. Then Melissa and Logan could get in touch with Griffin about what to do with Luthor.

"*After* the Showdown?" Mary Catherine echoed in consternation. "Don't you think we'll be a little busy between now and then? Like, *performing*?"

"We can hide him in one of the cabins," Bobby suggested.

Logan shook his head. "No good. The farmer is already nosing around. The dog has to stay where we can keep an eye on him."

"Why not right up onstage with us?" Mary Catherine's voice oozed sarcasm. "I'm sure nobody will notice a giant Doberman in the middle of everything. Don't all theatrical productions have some random dog just standing there for no reason at all?"

And then Melissa was staring right at it. "Pride Rock!" she exclaimed.

In the back corner of the Showdown stage sat a miniature mountain built atop a large rolling cart. In *The Lion King* sequence, that was where Rafiki the baboon held up the newborn baby Simba for all the animals to admire. Since it was so big, Pride Rock remained on the platform off in the wings throughout both revues. Right before "Hakuna Matata," the Ta-da! stagehands would wheel it out into the lights.

The curtain of hair was parted now, and Melissa's eyes were alight with excitement and purpose. "We'll hide him under Pride Rock. No one would ever think to lift up a giant set."

"It's perfect," Logan agreed. "The audience won't even know he's there."

A trickle of drool worked its way out of the corner of Luthor's mouth.

Moving like a giant amoeba with Luthor as its nucleus, the group shuffled across the compound, heading for the stage.

"Stay close together," Logan advised. "Keep him hidden."

Mary Catherine rolled her eyes. "Look who's turned into the big director all of a sudden. Mr. I'm-Too-Good-To-Play-a-Warthog."

At one point, they passed so close to the driver with the spiky hair that the man said, "Get out of my way, kids. I'm busy." But he never spotted the Doberman in their midst. It was a good thing Luthor had taken that partial hit from the tranquilizer dart. Had he been awake and alert, there would have been no way to contain his raucous, energetic movements and loud bark.

Oozing along a few inches at a time, the trip to the stage seemed to take forever. At last, the cluster curled around behind the platform to the backstage area and climbed up the steps.

It took several campers to tilt up one side of Pride Rock. Melissa took hold of Luthor's collar and urged him toward the hiding place.

For the first time since taking the dart, Luthor showed some resistance. This dark, cave-like space didn't seem like somewhere he wanted to be.

She removed one of the burgers from her pocket and placed it on the wooden stage under Pride Rock. Luthor followed it in, opened his huge jaws for a bite, and promptly fell asleep, the food still in his mouth.

"Is he going to behave in there?" asked Mary Catherine dubiously.

"Oh, sure," said Melissa. "He's a big softie."

This time it was the truth. Luthor *was* a softie— under the influence of a tranquilizer dart.

26

Twenty-five miles to the west, the same sun that shone on the Showdown reflected off the glassy surface of Ebony Lake. Long, narrow canoes dotted the water as far as the eye could see.

Savannah Drysdale was rowing in unison with her boatmates when her phone vibrated against the fabric of her bathing suit. She reached under her lifejacket, took out the handset, and squinted to read the small screen.

From: Melissa
Emergency! Luthor's location compromised, two dognappers at Ta-da! Luthor grazed by tranq. dart. Awaiting instructions.

In shock, Savannah squeezed the unit so hard that it squirted out of her grip, and she very nearly fumbled it overboard.

"Savannah!" her counselor admonished from the

front of the craft. "You're not supposed to have that here! Put it away before you ruin it!"

"S-s-sorry!" She stuffed the handset back under the life jacket, but she didn't care about any phone! All that mattered was Luthor!

Her sweet, loyal best friend in the world was in danger. And where was she? Twenty-five miles away, floating around like a useless idiot!

Where was Griffin? He had to be told about this immediately!

She looked frantically around the lake. He was in one of the many other canoes, but which one?

She needed The Man With The Plan.

The visiting camp was nothing short of phenomenal.

Spotlight's revue barreled along at rocket-ship velocity, shifting from large-scale musical set pieces to powerful dramatic scenes to hilarious comedy sketches. It was so entertaining that even the Ta-da! campers and counselors couldn't help but enjoy it.

Logan took every smattering of applause, every chuckle, every ooh or aah like a blow to the head with a baseball bat. "We're toast," he predicted mournfully. "Even if we *hadn't* broken into Mickey Bonaventure's house and accused him of dognapping, we wouldn't have a prayer." He gestured down the grassy slope, where the judge reclined in a lawn chair, smiling, clapping, and watching in rapt attention.

Melissa's focus was on the stage — not on the

actors, but on Pride Rock, off to the side. "So far so good. Nobody's noticed Luthor."

"Like things could be worse!" Logan moaned. "By the end of the day, Mickey Bonaventure's going to make sure that everybody on Spotlight has an agent! And us? *'Well, there was some guy in a warthog suit who showed some promise, but I never really saw his face.'*"

"This isn't about you," Melissa reminded him. She checked her phone. "I've already got twenty-three missed calls from Savannah!"

Logan nodded sheepishly. "We scored with the hiding place. Even if those two guys knew exactly where he was, they'd have to pull him out from under a rock in front of three hundred people."

The grand finale of the Spotlight revue was a medley from *Glee* that involved the entire cast. It drew grudging cheers from a Ta-da! crowd that would truly have loved the performance to bomb. A few were even on their feet, dancing to the music. At the end, Mickey Bonaventure himself stood up and snapped a salute to the triumphant cast.

"Okay, everybody!" Mary Catherine was smiling, but it was obvious that the quality of the Spotlight performance had displeased her mightily. "It's our turn now."

There was a twenty-minute break for the Spotlight campers to get out of costume and makeup, and to set up the stage for the Ta-da! home team. Soon the visitors were settled in the audience position on the grassy slope, and Wendy was giving her campers a last-minute pep talk.

"All right, they were great. We're great, too! Don't worry about topping Spotlight. Let's just do our thing, and we'll be amazing!"

There was a muffled snore, which everybody but Wendy knew was coming from beneath Pride Rock.

Melissa breathed deeply and took her place at the computer she had programmed to run the special effects. In her pocket, she felt her phone vibrate. Another call from Savannah, number thirty-something. She felt bad about leaving her friend hanging, but nothing could be done about it. There was no way she could take a call here, just as there had been no way she could take it in the audience during Spotlight's revue. And anyway, what could she possibly say to put Savannah's mind at rest?

"All right, places, everybody!" barked Mary Catherine.

Melissa punched the keyboard, and the opening music of *You're a Good Man, Charlie Brown* blasted out of the speaker. The actors marched out onstage, with the exception of Logan, who was playing Snoopy, and had to crawl on all fours.

The countless hours of rehearsal had paid off. The timing was crisp, the voices were clear, and the staging was excellent. From the many faces in the audience, Melissa sought out Mickey Bonaventure. She understood instantly that, although Ta-da! was good, they were not good enough to win the Showdown. The judge was sitting back, smiling politely, yet not with the enthusiasm he had shown the Spotlight cast. Or maybe it was her imagination. She was a computer geek. What did she know about theatre?

The sequence of scenes had become familiar to her by now. A song from *Cats*; a reading from *Twelfth Night*; a scene from *Miss Saigon*; poetry from *The Belle of Amherst*. *The Phantom of the Opera* was their mid-revue climax. Logan had no part in that number, so he joined Melissa at the mechanism that would bring down the "chandelier." He had already put on his warthog costume for "Hakuna Matata," which was coming up next. It was hard to take him seriously with his head protruding from Pumbaa's mouth. But the middle of the Showdown was not the time to point that out.

"How do you think it's going?" Melissa whispered.

"Mickey Bonaventure hates it," Logan replied morosely.

"I saw him clapping a couple of times," she protested.

"Probably swatting at mosquitoes. Trust me. If we don't *kill* from here on, we're doomed."

All at once, Melissa put an iron grip on his arm. "Look—"

He followed her gaze. Standing at the top of the hill, behind the audience, the two bus drivers were watching the show.

"Do you think they know?" she asked in a small voice.

"Not unless they've got X-ray vision," Logan replied. "How could they know?"

"Deductive reasoning," Melissa insisted. "They've scoured every millimeter of the camp. He isn't there, so he must be here. And when they see you onstage, they'll know you're involved with hiding the dog."

"Oh, yeah, like they'll recognize me in this outfit!" Logan scoffed. "My own mother couldn't find me with a telescope."

The song was ending, and the big moment was upon them. Melissa threw the switch, and Logan guided the rope upward. There were screams from the crowd as the "chandelier" toppled over the lighting arc and came down to the stage with an earsplitting crash.

A surge of applause swept in from the crowd.

For Melissa, the non-performer, it was her first chance to bask in the approval of an appreciative audience. Her eyes gleamed. "They liked it!"

"They loved it!" Logan agreed fervently. "Even Mickey Bonaventure! Hand me my caterpillars! We're still in this thing!"

What happened next was completely unexpected: Pride Rock moved.

27

"Did you see that?" Logan hissed.

Melissa had turned to stone. "Never mind me! Did the dognappers see it?"

Light dawned on Logan. "The crash from the chandelier—" He rushed around to the back of the stage and tried to peer under the rolling cart that formed the base of Pride Rock. To his dismay, he saw four canine legs standing upright. Luthor was awake.

Logan tried to press his cheek to the stage for a better view, but Pumbaa's head was too bulky. He caught a fleeting glimpse of the famished Luthor wolfing down the burger he'd fallen asleep with. Logan thought of the food he had stashed away in his pockets, and tried to reach inside the warthog suit. The costume simply wouldn't permit it. He would have to take the whole thing off, and put it back on again—too risky with "Hakuna Matata" coming up any minute.

"Melissa!" he exclaimed. "I need your burgers!"

She was amazed. "You're hungry *now*?"

"Not me — Luthor! If we feed him, maybe he'll go back to sleep."

But it was not to be. Mary Catherine, already in her lion outfit, came up and said, "What are you waiting for? Wheel Pride Rock into position!"

Uh-oh. "Are you sure it's the right time?" Logan stammered.

The Ta-da! captain's eyes shot sparks. "Of course it's the right time! Did you hear that ovation? We're catching fire! We have to keep it going!"

She and two wildebeest began to ease the rolling cart out toward center stage. Logan had a nightmare vision of Luthor overturning the set in full view of the audience and two professional dognappers. If the Doberman had the strength to move the heavy piece on his own, he could probably topple it. Without hesitation, Logan flung himself aboard Pride Rock. He landed flat on his face and, if it hadn't been for the soft material of the warthog costume, would probably have knocked himself unconscious against the wood of the set. When his vision cleared, he found himself high above the crowd, the object of everyone's attention.

Because it was unprofessional to waste stage time doing absolutely nothing, Logan made a great show of eating a caterpillar with much loud smacking of warthog lips. From the back row, the two bus drivers were staring directly at him. Still, no way could they know the dog was under the set.

"Get off!" Mary Catherine rasped from below.

It was a theatrical problem. Pumbaa was not supposed to be on top of Pride Rock in *The Lion King*. But Logan couldn't move without something else to weigh down the set. He could already feel Luthor scrambling around underneath the cart. It was time for an ad lib. He threw his head back and announced, "I think that baboon is coming up here to show everybody the new baby lion!"

There was a bit of a stir backstage, because this was definitely not in the script. But eventually, the actors were in place, and Rafiki the baboon, flanked by King Mufasa and his wife, climbed to the top of Pride Rock.

Mary Catherine was playing Queen Sarabi, and as Logan tried to retreat from the set, she elbowed him hard in the ribs and muttered, "You're dead, Kellerman!"

The camper playing Rafiki held up the stuffed toy representing the infant Simba, and cried, "Animals of the Pride Lands, behold your future king!"

A cheer went up from the cast, matched by one from the audience. It obscured a mournful howl that came from inside Pride Rock. Luthor was still groggy, but he seemed to be coming out of his partially tranquilized state. And that was bad news all around.

Logan wriggled off the scenery and found Melissa at the computer. "Luthor's definitely awake, and he must be hungry! Quick, give me your hamburgers! Maybe some food will calm him down!"

The two looped around the back of the stage and crawled out, hidden from the audience's view by the bulk of Pride Rock. Melissa unwrapped a burger and squeezed it under the gap between the rolling set and the platform. Another half inch would have cost her two fingers. The food was sucked in and snapped up in the blink of an eye.

"I've only got one more!" she warned.

"Give it to him! Give it to him!" It was almost time for "Hakuna Matata." Pumbaa was due onstage in less than a minute. "I've got a bunch more in my pocket! Can you reach inside my costume, and—"

Too late. Timon and the adolescent Simba had already taken the stage. "Hurry up!" Bobby hissed in his meerkat suit. "And don't forget your caterpillars!"

Logan knew he was out of options. With everything going on, and all the factors that needed his attention, one simple truth shone through everything: *The show must go on.* For Logan Kellerman, that rule was as basic and unchanging as the law of gravity.

So Pumbaa joined Timon and Simba in front of the audience. Logan could feel the bus drivers' eyes boring four laser holes in his costume. But he put that out of his mind, and sang his heart out, popping caterpillars and burping in all the right places as befitted a gassy warthog.

Mary Catherine the Klingon had done everything in her power to make him a nobody in this show. Well, maybe he couldn't change the casting, but there were no small roles, only small actors. And his Pumbaa would have the audience feeling the stomach cramps and tasting the wriggling bugs in the back of their throats.

And then Pride Rock rolled up and bumped him from behind.

The food hadn't calmed Luthor down. He was more restless than ever. Still singing, Logan leaned back against the set, and tried to wheel it away from the edge of the stage. The last thing they needed was for Pride Rock to go over the apron and take out the first three rows! Mickey Bonaventure would definitely deduct points for that.

The final chorus had never lasted longer. The audience must have noticed that Pumbaa did not join Timon and Simba for their dance, and instead leaned against the rock, pressing down with all his might. It wasn't great theatre but, when at last the cast pushed Pride Rock off into its corner, he sensed they were in the clear.

"Keep Luthor under there!" he called to Melissa, "no matter what happens!"

"Mary Catherine says hurry up and change," she advised. "You and Bobby are the last two for 'Gettysburg'!"

"I'm on it!" he promised.

A small tent had been set up backstage to serve as the wardrobe room. Bobby had thrown off his Timon costume and was about to don the long frock coat and stovepipe hat of Abraham Lincoln when Logan dashed inside, stripping out of Pumbaa.

"What's going on, Logan? Why is Pride Rock moving?"

"The dog woke up," Logan explained breathlessly. "And the farmer has two guys at the Showdown, looking for him. Mary Catherine needs to talk to you right away about what we're going to do!"

The trusting Bobby rushed out in search of the Ta-da! captain.

Grim with determination, Logan crammed himself into the President's black frock coat and trousers. He felt bad about tricking Bobby, who was a nice kid, even though he had no talent. But this was necessary. The Ta-da! revue had started off in the toilet, yet he could tell from the judge's eyes that the second half had brought steady improvement. They were in striking distance. He could taste it. But they needed an Abraham Lincoln who could bring the house down. It called for a touch of Kellerman magic.

He put on the fake beard and stovepipe hat, and checked his reflection in the mirror. A jarring note: The burgers in his pocket made him look fat, and Lincoln was anything but. Still, he couldn't dump the burgers. They might be needed to keep Luthor quiet.

Where could he stash them?

In a moment of inspiration, he stuffed them into the tall stovepipe hat, and crammed it tightly onto his head. Perfect. No one would ever know there were hamburgers up there. It might even help his posture look more presidential.

Bobby came rushing in. "Mary Catherine didn't — Logan, why are you wearing my costume?"

There could be no reasonable explanation, so Logan just ran out of the tent and took the stage. The Union soldiers seemed a little bewildered to see the wrong Lincoln standing there. So he launched right into, *"Four score and seven years ago our fathers . . ."*

It was a little fast and energetic for a man with smallpox, so he slowed down and mopped his brow with a handkerchief, being careful not to dislodge his hat. He could feel Mickey Bonaventure's eyes on him. This was it! He was doing it! He was winning over a real Hollywood actor!

A rumble like thunder shook the stage. In that instant, Logan realized that the judge hadn't been looking at him, but at Pride Rock, which was vibrating like a volcano about to blow. Two black-and-tan paws appeared in the gap between set and floor.

"Now we are engaged in a great civil war, testing whether that nation . . ."

Pride Rock rocked. It bounced once, slammed back to the platform, and then tilted up again, teetered there, and finally tipped over.

28

L uthor came roaring across the stage like he'd been launched by a catapult. He gamboled all around Logan, leaping and barking.

The audience was thunderstruck. Was this part of the show? And if so, what version of the Gettysburg Address had Mr. Lincoln being attacked by a giant dog?

"The brave men, living and dead, who struggled here . . ." It was the greatest challenge any actor could possibly face—to deliver a classic speech while fighting off a wild beast. Logan never wavered, and he never blew a line. Mickey Bonaventure couldn't have done it! Not even Johnny Depp! When Luthor knocked the hat off and the hamburgers came tumbling down, Logan didn't falter. He finished with ". *. . government of the people, by the people, for the people, shall not perish from the earth."* Luthor stood beside him, his large snout buried in the pile of fallen food.

Mickey Bonaventure leaped to his feet, applauding

and howling with laughter. With him rose the entire audience, including the competition from Camp Spotlight. This was a comedy routine without equal.

Melissa didn't know much about drama, but she understood instantly that Logan had just put Camp Ta-da! in position for the greatest come-from-behind win in Showdown history. So she cued the music for the final number of the revue—the song "Tomorrow" from the Broadway show *Annie*.

Mary Catherine was beside herself. "We can't do the finale now! The show's ruined!"

"No, it's not!" Melissa insisted. "We're a smash! Look!"

It was true. Logan was taking bows, basking in the glory of his standing ovation.

Melissa put the curly red wig on Mary Catherine's head. "You go out and sell this song, and we're winners for sure!"

It had to be the first time all summer that Mary Catherine did what someone else told her to do, without putting up an argument. She walked to the center of the stage, took a deep breath, and inhaled a few stray hairs from Luthor. Her allergies kicked in.

Mary Catherine Klinger dissolved into fits of sneezing that had no end. It was so violent and so loud that, for a moment, Luthor looked away from his food. The audience watched, transfixed. Was this another surprise comedy routine? Should they laugh?

Standing in the wings, Melissa was frozen with indecision. They were going to lose the Showdown because of Mary Catherine's allergies!

Before Melissa fully understood what she was doing, she was striding across the stage in front of all those people. If there was one thing she didn't relish, it was being the center of attention. Yet she had to do this — not for Mary Catherine, who had been horrible to Logan, and none too pleasant to everybody else. This was for the Ta-da! performers, who had worked so hard. It was even for herself, to prove that she could do it, so she could retire undefeated and never do it again.

Melissa took the wig from Mary Catherine and placed it on her own head. Then she stood beside Luthor, and began to sing.

"The sun will come out tomorrow,
Bet your bottom dollar that tomorrow
there'll be sun . . ."

Strong, full, and clear as a bell, the voice that came from behind the curtain of hair was not to be believed. It seemed to soar over the outdoor auditorium, leaving the spectators unmoving and transfixed.

Lincoln's hat dropped from Logan's nerveless fingers, and he didn't even notice, so enthralled was he with his friend's performance. Mary Catherine stared, openmouthed, at the girl who had absolutely refused to sing. Luthor stopped eating and listened, as if hypnotized.

Her eyes squeezed shut, the star of the moment noticed none of this, so petrified was shy Melissa at being the object of such total focus. In her mind, she was not singing; she was repairing a fried computer circuit board. As the powerful melody swelled from her throat, she was painstakingly working with a tiny tweezers, reattaching color-coded wires to gold-plated connectors. It was the only thing preventing her from passing out from sheer stage fright.

She finished the number and opened her eyes to make sure the world hadn't ended during her ordeal. There was stunned silence, broken only by Mary Catherine's wheezing. Then waves of rapturous applause flooded the stage.

"I declare Camp Ta-da! the winners!" shouted Mickey Bonaventure over the noise.

The response was nothing short of pandemonium. The entire Ta-da! cast swarmed the stage, bumping the upended Pride Rock and knocking it back on its base again. The counselors were right behind them, escorting a sheepish but triumphant Bobby, who was wrapped in a blanket.

Logan enfolded Mary Catherine in an ecstatic bear hug. She sneezed in his face, but looked very pleased to accept the trophy as the winning captain. It was a celebration three years in the making, and it was all the more joyous because it had taken so long to come to pass.

The Spotlight visitors, good sports in the end, joined the cheers.

Amid the chaos, Melissa glanced down and noticed something that very nearly stopped her heart. Luthor was no longer by her side. Frantic, she looked around. There was the elder of the two bus drivers, slinking through the partying throng, leading Luthor at the end of his leash.

Melissa was a quiet person, but her solo had twisted her volume control to maximum. She used every decibel now. *"It's the farmer! He's taking the dog! Stop him!"*

The dognapper never had a chance. The campers were on him in an instant, knocking him to the ground and sitting on him. Athena wrenched the leash from his hand and tossed it to Melissa. She caught it—just in time to see the other driver, the one with the spiky hair, pushing through the crowd toward her.

Her eyes met Logan's. Neither of them was The Man With The Plan, but they had been friends with Griffin long enough to recognize a classic Code Z when they saw one. The jig was up, and it was time to get Luthor away from there.

They leaped off the back of the stage and made for the trees, Luthor loping along beside them. They had not yet reached cover when Spiky Hair broke free of the chaos in hot pursuit.

"Where are we going?" Logan rasped.

"It doesn't matter," she panted in reply, "so long as we can lose this guy, hunker down, and call Griffin and Savannah!"

"What if they don't answer their phones?"

"I've got seventy-four missed calls," Melissa gasped. "I'm pretty sure they'll pick up!"

29

The logo on the Chevy Silverado read NORTH COUN-TRY POOL COMPANY. Rattling east on the bumpy road, the driver had no idea that he had two unofficial passengers lying under a tarpaulin in his flatbed.

Savannah was practically hysterical. "Why don't they answer? What's happened to them? What's happened to Luthor?"

Griffin was worried, too, but he knew that panic could only jeopardize the plan. "If you don't stop calling, you're going to drain your battery. We'll know soon enough. I'm pretty sure we're almost there."

Cautiously, the two poked their heads out of the tarp and peered over the side wall of the flatbed. An amazing sight greeted their eyes. Coming toward them, running full-tilt along the dirt shoulder, were Logan, Melissa, and Luthor. Griffin was just about to call out to them as they flashed by, when he caught sight of their pursuer, a young man with spiky hair.

Savannah did not hesitate to act in defense of her beloved dog. She picked up the long-handled bug dipper, raised herself to her knees, and brought it down like a butterfly net just as the pickup passed Spiky Hair. Her aim was perfect. The netting stopped his head, and the rest of him wiped out on the shoulder and rolled down into the ditch. His cry of shock was so loud that the pool man screeched to a halt and jumped from the truck, thinking that he'd hit someone.

Griffin and Savannah hopped out of the flatbed and took off along the road after their fleeing friends.

Even at full gallop, Luthor picked up Savannah's scent on the wind. He made a U-turn so tight that it would have jackknifed a tractor trailer. In an instant, he was in Savannah's arms, being hugged, kissed, and fussed over.

The four friends met by the edge of the trees.

"Run!" Logan choked. "There's a guy after us!"

"Old news," Griffin soothed. "Savannah took care of him."

"Why didn't you tell us you were coming?" Melissa panted.

"Why didn't you answer your phone?" Savannah countered.

"It's complicated," Melissa tried to explain. "We're Code Z now, Griffin. Luthor's compromised. He can't stay here anymore."

"That's why we came," Griffin confirmed. "We've still got one secure location left. Pitch and Ben are at

Camp Endless Pines. It's only another twenty miles down the road."

"How are you going to get there?" Logan pointed to the pool truck, which was disappearing down the road. "There goes your transportation."

Griffin grinned. "I've memorized the schedule for all the delivery guys up here. The bakery van should be coming through in half an hour or so. Don't worry about us. Everything's part of the plan."

Their rendezvous was brief. Logan and Melissa knew that they had to get back to camp before anyone missed them. They were the two biggest stars of the Showdown — Comedy Abe Lincoln and Annie who sang with all the exquisite yearning of a young orphan girl.

Back at Ta-da!, the revelry was winding down, and the visitors were climbing back aboard their buses for the trip home to Spotlight.

Logan and Melissa received countless high fives, and even scattered applause. They were no longer the camp losers who had fought with the captain and alienated the judge. Everybody knew they were the two performers who had put Ta-da! over the top.

"Ah — there you are." Mickey Bonaventure came over to them. "I just wanted to let you know that I have no hard feelings for what happened between us." He turned to Melissa. "In all my professional experience, I have never heard 'Tomorrow' sung so beautifully, even on Broadway. Congratulations. And you" — to Logan — "that was the most creative, unexpected, hilarious performance I've ever witnessed. I'm going to tell everyone I know in Hollywood to be on the lookout for Ferris Atwater, Jr." And he melted into the crowd.

"No! Wait! I'm not Atwater, I'm Kellerman! K—E—" He made to run after the judge, but his way was blocked by two very angry bus drivers. The older man was limping heavily. The younger man's spiky hair was considerably flattened. As well, his face was mottled by a fine mesh pattern, a souvenir of his sudden meeting with the bug dipper.

"All right!" growled the man with the bad leg. "Where's the dog?"

Logan drew himself to his full height, looked the man square in the face, and said, "What dog?" It was so outrageous that even Melissa stared at him in disbelief. Half an hour ago, the Doberman had been center stage in front of hundreds of people.

Spiky Hair's face reddened. "Don't give me that! Where'd you stash the pooch?"

Logan stood firm. "Sorry, I really don't know what you're talking about."

"We're all loaded up," called the Spotlight head counselor from behind them. "Let's go."

"You haven't heard the last of me!" the older man promised as the two drivers reluctantly retreated to their buses.

"Wow!" breathed Melissa. "Where'd you get the nerve to stand three feet away from two professional criminals and lie to their faces when we all know there *was* a dog?"

"It wasn't lying," Logan replied honestly. "It was *acting.*"

"Acting?"

"I was portraying a character who *hadn't* seen a dog. Listen, Melissa, you're a genius at computers, and I guess you're pretty good at singing, too. But you've got a lot to learn about the theatre. Any bunch of idiots can put on a decent show if they practice hard enough. But to tell two hired goons there's no dog after they found him, shot him, chased him, and almost got him in the end—now, *that's* a performance!"

From: Griffin
To: Ben
On our way. Get ready for Operation Hideout:
Phase Three.

THE THIRD HIDEOUT

30

Camp Endless Pines was aptly named. Located in rugged, hilly terrain, the coniferous forest stretched in all directions as far as the eye could see.

Ben just called it Camp Endless. If it had been up to him, he never would have signed up for a program that was so hipped on outdoor adventure activities — hiking, rafting, caving, parasailing, wind surfing — a guy could break his neck just reading the list! And that didn't even include the climbing! Mountain scrambles, top roping, Alpine training, bouldering. It was fine for Antonia "Pitch" Benson, who was practically born with a carabiner for a diaper pin. She and her whole family were big-time rock-jocks.

Ben Slovak was here for exactly one reason. Camp Endless was the only summer camp that would accept Ferret Face. And without the little ferret under Ben's shirt giving him strategic wake-up nips, there would be no way to keep Ben's narcolepsy under control. The last thing he needed was to fall asleep in the middle of a camp activity like canoeing, or a hike. An unscheduled nap was annoying enough at home. In the wilderness it could be fatal.

The choice had become Endless Pines or nothing. And Mr. and Mrs. Slovak had made it very clear that nothing was not an option.

So here he was, climbing rocks and counting the minutes until he could go home.

How could it be worse? Ben wasn't sure. But he had a sinking feeling it had something to do with hiding a giant Doberman for the last ten days of camp.

Speaking of climbing, Pitch shinnied down the trunk of a tall pine and dropped at his feet.

"Well?" Ben queried. "Did you see the truck?"

"Not yet, but it can't be far. I think we should go out to the barrier. They could be along any minute."

The barrier was a huge limb, itself the size of a small tree. It had taken Pitch and Ben twenty minutes to drag it out where it would block the narrow dirt road. The job had been so stressful and sweaty that Ferret Face had tried to abandon his post inside Ben's T-shirt. The ferret had been a little less reliable lately. He wasn't enjoying Camp Endless any better than Ben was.

The two concealed themselves in the underbrush by the side of the road. That was another thing about this place. The minute you stepped outside the camp, you might as well have been a thousand miles from the nearest other human.

"You know," Pitch said conversationally, "the minute

I heard Luthor was going to Logan and Melissa, I knew it was only a matter of time before he ended up here with us."

"Do you think Swindle's spies will find him here?" Ben asked nervously. He couldn't imagine anyone finding "here," much less a single animal hidden here.

"They'll probably try," Pitch said grimly. "I hope The Man With The Plan has some really great ideas on how we can make this work, because we've officially run out of camps. I'd hate to see the poor mutt go back to Swindle."

"What I'm worried about is what Swindle's going to do once he's gotten rich off Luthor's dog-show skills. Remember, he's already promised to move back to Cedarville and devote his money to ruining our lives. I've got enough problems without some sleazy millionaire's revenge fantasy."

"None of it happens if we can keep the dog under wraps," Pitch reminded him in a soothing tone. "Wait— I think I hear something."

A motor, distant but unmistakable, was the only sound in the woods that wasn't coming from something gross rubbing its legs together.

The van appeared out of the trees, bouncing slowly along the rutted dirt road. It came to a stop in front of the fallen tree branch.

Ferret Face poked his head out of Ben's collar and looked on with interest. When the driver began the arduous task of hauling the heavy limb out of the way,

Pitch and Ben swung into action. They darted around to the back of the vehicle and opened the twin doors. Griffin, Savannah, and Luthor jumped down, and the five disappeared into the trees.

"Thanks, you guys!" Griffin greeted them. "Is everything prepared?"

"Nothing's prepared," Pitch said irritably. "You texted us barely an hour ago. What were we supposed to do — build a safe house?"

"The most important thing is to find somewhere for Luthor to hide," Savannah put in. "It should be comfortable, but not too obvious, close enough so you can bring him food and come to visit regularly, because the poor sweetie has just been through a terrible experience. He needs to feel loved."

"Is it okay if he just feels liked?" asked Pitch. "I can do liked."

"There aren't a lot of doghouse options around here," Ben warned. "We're lucky we have shelter for ourselves. This is a roughing-it kind of camp."

Griffin looked around. Tall trees stood like sentinels all about them. At last, they heard the bakery van continuing on its way, and the group ventured out of the woods to the relative openness of the road.

"What's that?" Griffin was pointing at what looked like a small hut towering over the top of the trees.

Pitch followed his gaze. "That's an old ranger station. Back in the day, they used to send a guy up there to scout for forest fires. But now that's done by heli-copter and satellite."

"So it's just empty?" Griffin probed.

"Wait a minute," Savannah interjected suspiciously. "You're not thinking of stashing Luthor a mile in the sky! How would you even get him up there?"

"Only one way to find out," Griffin decided.

Skirting the camp, the group made its way through the woods. The closer they got to the abandoned sta-tion, the taller it seemed, towering in the sky easily thirty feet clear of the highest treetop. At last, they reached its base, where a faded sign proclaimed: P OUT.

Griffin licked his finger and cleaned off the rest of the message. It now read: KEEP OUT.

"Is it safe?" asked Savannah dubiously. She stared at the steep, rickety steps that spiraled up around the thick wooden support pole.

"Safer than turning Luthor over to Swindle," said Griffin briskly.

Savannah started up the stairs. "I'll go first."

It was a very tentative procession that made its way to the top of the ranger tower. Only Pitch, the climber, found the going easy. The others hugged the center pole, not daring to look down. Luthor whined and protested, and only Savannah's reassuring voice kept him putting one paw in front of the other. Ferret Face peeked out of Ben's sleeve, spotted the ground far below, and retreated with a terrified squeak.

At last, they reached the top and noted with relief that the platform was solid beneath their feet. There were no walls, although torn screening still enclosed most of the space. A lot of bugs had made their way in, and at least one family of birds was nesting beneath the roof. But the shelter was basically dry. Best of all, it seemed like the last place on earth anyone would look for a fugitive Doberman.

Then came the hard part — convincing Luthor that he had to part with his beloved Savannah yet again. For the first time, the dog seemed angry, even when Savannah used her best dog-whispering voice. He seemed to be saying, *I've done my part, several times, and this is asking too much of me.*

Savannah was brokenhearted. "I'll stay here with him!" she quavered.

"Don't be crazy!" Griffin argued. "If either one of us isn't back at Ebony Lake by bed check, there'll be a big stink, and everything's going to get found out, including Luthor's whereabouts. And that's his one-way ticket to Swindle."

"I just feel so bad for him." Savannah sniffled. "He's been such a trouper through all this! And what do we do? We ask him for more sacrifice!"

Luthor lay down on the floor, glaring at them resentfully, his hot breath moving the cobwebs that decorated every corner.

"Actually, he seems pretty cool with it," Ben pointed out. "I mean, he's bummed, but he isn't barking or anything."

"This is a hundred times worse than barking," said Savannah reproachfully. "He's given me his trust, and I've betrayed him. He may never forgive me."

"For crying out loud," Pitch exclaimed, exasperated, "he's a *dog*. He'll forgive you with the first Puppy Treat."

"You know," Griffin put in, "we should really get moving if we're going to make the next laundry truck west."

"I know it's not easy, sweetie," Savannah pleaded with the Doberman. "But this is the only way."

Luthor looked daggers at her as she clipped his leash around the platform railing. A low growl began deep in his throat.

Savannah was devastated. "He hasn't growled at me since his old guard dog days! What if, in trying to keep him from Swindle, we're turning him back into the mean, antisocial animal he used to be?"

"We're not just protecting Luthor," Ben reasoned. "We're derailing Swindle's revenge before it ever starts, and that saves all our necks."

Griffin put a sympathetic arm around his friend's shoulders, and started her down the stairs out of the station. "One thing at a time. First we hide him, then we worry about you two guys making friends again."

Following them around the spiral, Ben had a practical question for Pitch. "How are we ever going to look after that dog? If Savannah gets growled at, the two of us will be lunch!"

It was going to be a really long ten days.

B en, wake up."
     Ben opened one eye. It was still dark, which
meant he was obviously dreaming. No, he could make
out the first faint colors of dawn creeping in the windows of Cabin 17. Eli, the counselor, reached out and
poked him in the ribs. "Come on, Ben. Everybody's
ready except you!"

"Ready for what? It's the middle of the night!"

"No, it isn't. It's five-fifteen!" Eli insisted. "The fish
are biting!"

That was another thing that was big at Camp
Endless, along with cliff climbing and kayaking over
waterfalls: getting up at oh-dark-thirty to go fishing.

Ferret Face peeked out from under the blanket and
glared at the counselor, yellow eyes glowing. Waking
Ben up was *his* job, and he was protective of it.

Eli backed off. "Oh, I get it. You're too tired, right?"

As the only camper with a sleep disorder, Ben was
cut a lot of slack in that department.

"You get some more rest, Ben. I'll ask one of the guys to look in on you in a couple of hours." The rest of the bunk clattered out with their fishing gear, hip waders squeaking.

"No, Ferret Face," Ben said irritably as the small animal climbed inside his pajama top. "It's not time to get up yet." He tried to settle back in his bunk, but Ferret Face delivered one of his trademark wake-up nips. "Ow! Okay, okay, I'm getting up! Sheesh!"

Ben peered out the small window in the cabin. Aside from his own bunkmates, not a creature was stirring. The mess hall was still dark, so breakfast wasn't an option. Last night after lights-out, Pitch had climbed the ranger tower with food and water for Luthor, so he was taken care of for the time being. With his bunkmates out of the picture, Ben should probably sneak over and check in on the Doberman. But the thought of going up those stairs in the half-light with no Pitch wasn't very appealing.

So he took out his phone and decided to tap out an e-mail to his parents:

Dear Mom and Dad,
    I'm writing this by the light of the fire from last night's asteroid strike. The whole camp is destroyed, but don't worry. The smoke keeps the bears away. . . .

Obviously, his parents weren't going to believe this,

just as they hadn't believed the volcano, the tsunami, or the zombie apocalypse. But they were definitely getting the message, which was that their son didn't like camp very much.

Unfortunately, the National Guard is rescuing us in alphabetical order. I'm not sure I'll be still alive by the time they make it to S. At least I'm not Matthew Ziegelbaum, who is writing his will even as we speak.

Well, gotta go. They're toasting marshmallows over the flaming latrine. I wouldn't want to miss out on that. It might be the last food I'll ever eat.

With his finger hovering over SEND, Ben frowned. What was that cooking smell? Maybe someone *was* roasting marshmallows. No, this was more like steak. Was he imagining it?

Ferret Face popped out from under his collar and sniffed the air.

"Steak, right?"

In answer, the furry creature scurried down the length of Ben's body, scampered across the floor, and slithered out the crack under the door in pursuit of the tantalizing aroma.

"Hey, come back here!" But it was too late. The ferret was already gone.

Tossing the phone onto the bed, Ben headed off in pursuit. What a time for Ferret Face to go on one of his little walkabouts—in unfamiliar surroundings where he could easily get lost, or forget which of the identical cabins was the right one. And who knew what kind of animal might prey on a tame little guy like him? Ferrets weren't at the bottom of the food chain, but they weren't at the top, either.

Uh-oh. A yawn confirmed it. Ben could feel the irresistible drowsiness stealing into him like a blanket coming down over his head. And this time there were no little sharp teeth to shock him back to awareness. When narcolepsy struck, there usually wasn't time to make it to a chair or a couch. He didn't collapse, exactly. But it was all he could do to reach the wall, where he slid down to a seated position on the floor, snoring softly, dead to the world.

Dominic Hiller was flat broke. The steak alone had cost him $26.95, not to mention the gas money for a thirty-mile round-trip to the nearest diner. This whole job was turning out to be one disaster after another. His leg hurt from when all those kids jumped on him at the other camp. His partner had quit outright, telling Mr. Palomino, "It's not worth it! These aren't regular kids! They're some kind of doomsday machine!" And on top of it all, it was starting to rain. These dirt roads would be pure mud by the time he found the dog and got him to the rendezvous point.

He squinted at the number on the cabin—17. According to the camp records, that was where the

Slovak kid was. If Palomino's theory was right and Luthor had been passed to Slovak, then the mutt was hidden here somewhere, within smelling distance of a big, juicy twenty-seven-dollar steak!

Come on, pooch. Come to Papa.

At that moment, a bundle of fur burst through the cabin door and made a beeline for the meat.

For a split second, Hiller actually allowed himself to think, *Hey, this is easy!* before he noticed that the animal gnawing crazily on the bait was about one-eight-hundredth the size of Luthor. He reached out to brush the interloper away. The little weasel-like creature sank tiny razor-sharp teeth into his hand, drawing blood. The effort to keep from screaming brought tears to his eyes. Sucking air, he kicked the steak a few yards away. The animal released his hand and scrambled off after it.

Where was the mutt? He shone a flashlight under Cabin 17, then eased the door a crack and peered inside. There was only one kid in there—fast asleep on the floor—and no dog. Camp sure was different from when he'd been a kid.

A phone sat on a bunk, its screen still lit. That was weirder yet! The kid must have been typing less than sixty seconds ago. Who goes to sleep that fast? And on the floor? He picked up the phone. There was a half-finished e-mail on the screen from sender *Slovak, Benjamin*. So this was definitely the right kid.

What to do, then? Squeeze the dog's location out of Slovak? Or . . .

He opened the phone's camera function, and there it was: the most recent picture was Luthor, standing on a screen porch somewhere. No, make that a balcony, a high one — the trees were far below. He clicked on another photo, and light dawned. The "balcony" — he'd seen it before. It was the fire-spotting platform just west of the camp. He'd passed it on the way in. That was where they'd stashed the dog!

He covered the bite wound with his mouth to soothe it. This might turn out to be easy after all.

32

Pitch loved climbing in the rain. Clothes turned damp and heavy, and could throw off your sense of balance. The rocks got wet, slippery, and treacherous. Dirt and gravel became loose and unstable. Best of all, most of the other climbers gave up and went home. That left just Pitch, alone with the rock face, the purest relationship in the world—the climber and the challenge.

The crest of the ridge was just a few feet above her now. She pushed for it, enjoying the burn in her muscles. This was always her favorite part—the moment when she reached the top, the highest point, and a whole new vista unfolded before her on the other side.

There was the camp, nestled in the pines. And, about three-quarters of a mile away, the ranger platform where Luthor was safe and sound . . . or was he?

There was a dark shape halfway up the steps on the tower. A person? It had to be. But the shape was kind of wrong, huge across the shoulders. Like Bigfoot wearing blue jeans! Whoever or whatever, it was descending very slowly, almost painfully.

She squinted for a clearer picture, but the platform was just too far away. Acting on pure instinct, she began to climb down the other side of the ridge, moving carefully, yet never taking her eyes off the mysterious figure. She continued to find lower and lower positions, steadying herself with handholds that were often little more than a single finger jammed into a tiny crack or hole. Most mountaineers spent years perfecting the techniques she had grown up with. In the Benson house, it was as natural as breathing.

The mysterious figure was on the ground now, stepping out of the shadow of the tower. All at once, Pitch was low enough to get a good look. It was a man, all right. The giant humpback resolved into a familiar expanse of black and tan fur.

Pitch's breath caught in her throat. This was Swindle's man! And he had Luthor slung over his shoulders!

Instinctively, she reached for her cell phone to alert Ben, but then realized she'd left it back in her cabin. No one climbed with a phone—not if they wanted it to be in one piece at the end of the day. She was on her own. If anything was going to be done, she would have to be the doer.

She sped up her descent. She was no planner, like Griffin. But what she lacked in strategy, she made up for in raw determination. She was going to stop this guy even if she had to tackle him into a tree! Then, hopefully, Luthor would protect her if the goon got mad. As she moved down the rock face, she wondered why Luthor hadn't protected himself, especially in view of yesterday's angry mood.

She'd find out soon enough — at least, she would if she got there in time.

Hurry up!

She worked her way around a rock spur, and noticed for the first time a mud-spattered red pickup pulled over to the side of the dirt road. It seemed to her that Luthor's kidnapper was heading there. If he made it to the truck . . .

The wet clay of a foothold disintegrated beneath her weight, and she dropped several feet, bruising her pride almost as much as her hindquarters. Dismayed, she found herself on a narrow ledge over a sheer drop. There was no way down from here. She had to climb up and around just to continue her descent.

Stupid!

She had cost herself time, and there was none to waste if she was going to beat Swindle's man to the pickup.

She realized too late that she wasn't going to make it. The jerk was already leaving the cover of the trees for the road. She was in an agony of guilt. She and Ben had been given Luthor less than twenty-four hours ago, and already they were losing him!

The man limped over to the pickup—he was walking with a cane, she noted. She could see clearly from this vantage point that the Doberman's eyes were shut, and his body was limp.

Tranquilized, she concluded. *Out cold.*

With effort, the man loaded the hundred-and-fifty pound dog into the backseat of the crew cab, and heaved himself in behind the wheel.

Pitch watched helplessly as the truck started up. The most she could do was try to read and memorize the license plate so they could report it to the police. But what use could that possibly be? A judge had legally awarded Luthor to Swindle. In the eyes of the law, this wasn't kidnapping. The real kidnapping had happened when Griffin and Savannah had smuggled Luthor to Ebony Lake in the first place. It was so unfair!

If Pitch had had time to think about what happened next, she never would have done it. The truck jounced along the muddy road, passing directly under her perch. She dropped fifteen feet straight into the payload, bouncing catlike off the truck bed, and falling back into a pile of tires. The beating of the rain, the roar of the motor, and the groaning of old shock absorbers over rough terrain masked the sound of impact. The driver never turned his head.

Luthor was in enemy hands, but he was not alone.

33

Ben felt like he was swimming upward through layer after layer of clinging fog. Even in his dazed state, he knew from bitter experience exactly what had happened to him. This was no regular sleep. This was—

"Ben!" Eli slapped him lightly on both cheeks. "Wake up, Ben! What happened to you? Why are you on the floor?"

The room came into focus at last. He saw his counselor and bunkmates leaning over him in concern. His first response was to pat at his T-shirt. Nobody home.

"Where's Ferret Face?" he demanded.

"Your weasel?" asked one boy, toweling off his wet hair. "He's just outside."

Ben struggled to his feet. No wonder he'd fallen asleep like that! Ferret Face was lying down on the job! He staggered to the door and threw it open. There was the little creature, languid and stuffed, still gnawing at a half-eaten steak.

"Oh, great!" Ben exclaimed. "When it comes down

to me or your stomach, we all know where *I* stand!" He frowned. "Eli, are they serving steak in the mess hall today?"

The counselor laughed. "Steak? At this place? Try Corn Flakes."

Stupid question. It was breakfast.

It was starting to come back to him. Right before he'd conked out, he distinctly remembered smelling steak.

Who brought steak to a summer camp at five in the morning? Someone who wanted to draw out an animal. And nobody wanted to draw out a ferret. That steak had been bait—for *Luthor*!

His reeling mind immediately reached two terrifying conclusions: (1) Swindle's agents had already tracked the Doberman to Camp Endless Pines, and (2) at least one of those agents had been right here in the last few hours.

Haunted, he scanned the compound, half expecting to see an enemy crouched behind every hut and building. He looked down. There were dozens of footprints in the mud, but one set stood out—two large construction boots flanked by a neat round hole, something made by a crutch or a cane. Yesterday Griffin had told them that one of Swindle's men had hurt his leg at the Ta-da! Showdown. It couldn't be a coincidence.

Ben snatched up the soggy Ferret Face and stuffed him inside his shirt. "Come on, little man. You've eaten enough." He had to call Pitch. This was a full-blown crisis.

Back inside, he found his phone lying on the floor, close to the spot where he'd napped. When he unlocked the screen, the image that appeared sent cold fingers of dread clutching at his heart. It was a picture he'd taken of the ranger station—Luthor's new safe haven. No way had he been looking at it this morning. Someone had checked his phone. If Swindle's man had seen this picture of Luthor at the ranger platform, then things were even worse than he'd feared.

He dialed Pitch's number. It went straight to voicemail. "We've got big trouble!" he recorded. "Call me right away!"

A half hour went by. No call.

He left a second message, this one practically hysterical.

While waiting for a response, he borrowed binoculars from the supply hut and trained them on the elevated ranger station. There was no sign of Luthor. There was no sign of any life up there.

But that doesn't necessarily mean anything. It's raining. Visibility's bad. I wouldn't see him if he was lying flat on the floor. Or maybe Pitch brought him down to go for a walk. And she isn't picking up because her phone got rained on. What am I getting so crazy about?

An hour went by. No sign of Luthor; no word from Pitch.

He went to her cabin, number two. No one had seen her since breakfast.

There was no getting away from it. He had to climb up that ranger tower to see if Luthor was there.

He told Eli he'd be in the Arts and Crafts tent, making a wallet, and then snuck out of the compound, heading for the station. All the way, he lectured Ferret Face. "It's, like, ninety feet straight up. And if I fall asleep on those stairs, I'm a dead man. So no goofing off. I mean it."

At last, he reached the base of the platform and began his ascent. As he neared the top, he called out, "Luthor? Pitch? Are you there?"

Silence.

With a sinking heart, he pulled himself up into the screened-in station. It was empty.

He sat down to catch his breath, broken with despair. He'd known he was going to find this, but somehow he'd been holding out the faint hope that he was wrong, that he'd misunderstood somehow, and that everything was really fine.

A tiny flash of yellow caught his eye. He moved to get a closer look. Embedded in a wooden post was a small feathered tranquilizer dart. And in the dust on the floor, evidence of a turbulent struggle, large canine paw prints along with construction boots and, yes, the imprint of a rubber-tipped crutch or cane. It was proof beyond a doubt that the worst-case scenario had come to pass.

Luthor had been kidnapped.

And Pitch? Where was Pitch?

Back on the ground, he picked up the trail in the mud of the forest floor. Heavier footsteps, deeper. Why? Because the man had been carrying a tranquilized one-hundred-fifty-pound dog! The prints went on for a short distance to the dirt road, where they disappeared. From that point, Luthor and his captor had driven away in some kind of vehicle. Probably a small truck. The tires were wide, and dug two distinct grooves into the mud of the dirt road.

He began to follow the tracks, while berating himself for doing such a stupid thing. The truck could have gone a hundred miles, maybe more. Was he going to walk that far? Yet, while there was a trail to follow, he couldn't bring himself to turn back. Futile as it seemed, it was just that important. He'd always rolled his eyes at Griffin's stubborn devotion to his plans. And here was Ben, the sensible one, doggedly pushing onward against all logic.

It was not loyalty to Griffin that kept his wet feet moving; not compassion for Luthor; not even so much his worry about Pitch, who, of the six team members, could take care of herself. It was this: Ben could not bear the thought of spending the rest of his life looking over his shoulder, waiting for Swindle's revenge. Better to stand up to their enemy now, even if that meant taking on the mud and the rain and the endless north woods.

He trudged along, never lifting his gaze from the tire tracks. Luckily, it was so early in the morning that the only fresh grooves deep in the mud belonged to the truck he was following. That wouldn't last as the day went on and more traffic appeared on this road. Not so lucky was the fact that he was soaked to the skin, and caked in slime up to the knees. If his mother could see him, she'd be running a hot bath and making oatmeal.

So absorbed was he in his own misery and the crisis at hand that he nearly walked past the bike. It was a rusty old wreck, probably from the 1970s because it had one of those long banana seats. Someone had obviously thrown it away, or it had fallen off a roof rack on its way to being thrown away. But the chain was still in place, and the fat tires seemed to have air. It looked pretty rickety, but it was better than walking.

It's not like I could get any wetter or dirtier by falling off a beat-up bike.

He got on, and began to wobble down the road, placing his front wheel in one of the ruts made by the getaway truck. An alarmed Ferret Face peered out of his collar and directed a quizzical look up at him.

"Don't ask," he muttered. There could be no good explanation for this, not even if he spoke ferret.

34

It was a rough ride, even for a rock climber. Pitch could feel her breakfast tossing around with every bump in the road. The tires, mudguards and all, were spraying her with a constant shower of slime. If it was possible to be less comfortable, she didn't see how.

She crouched in the front driver's-side corner of the flatbed, barely daring to move for fear that Swindle's man might catch a glimpse of her in the rearview mirror. From her spot, she could just spy the slumbering Luthor. At least, she hoped he was slumbering. He was awfully still.

She couldn't tell how far they'd gone when the pickup veered off the narrow, muddy, bumpy road onto an even narrower, muddier, bumpier side road. Her watch said they'd been traveling a little less than half an hour. When she dared to peek over the side wall, she could see they were approaching a tiny neat cottage. Sure enough, they pulled up onto a gravel front drive and parked.

Pitch pressed her body against the truck bed, holding herself as low as possible, so even if the man glanced at the payload, his eyes would pass right over her. Still, she was ready for instant action. If she had to escape, she could definitely outrun a man with a cane.

She needn't have worried. He checked briefly on Luthor, and then limped into the house.

Pitch was out of the truck bed in an instant, and into the backseat beside the Doberman.

"Okay, Luthor, rise and shine." There was absolutely no response. She placed her hand high up on his belly, and was relieved to feel a steady heartbeat and deep, even breathing. "Come on, big guy. I know you're tired, but it's time to bounce!"

Luthor wasn't bouncing. He was alive, but that was it.

With a sigh of resignation, she wrapped her arms around the dog's midsection and attempted to heave him bodily out of the cab. She felt his hundred-and-fifty-pound body move an inch or two, but then her strength was at an end, and she was setting him down again. She tried once more, if only because not trying was something a Benson would never accept. She might have been struggling like that all day if she hadn't heard an approaching engine. Frantically, she shut Luthor back in the cab and dove behind a stand of bushes near the front of the house.

The new vehicle came into view, shaking and bouncing even more violently than the pickup had. It, too, was mud to the axle, and the wipers labored at top speed, clearing the windshield of watery filth. It turned into the drive and parked behind the pickup.

Pitch had just an instant to reflect that the compact SUV bore stickers from a car rental company when the door opened, and out stepped S. Wendell Palomino.

That rotten Swindle was no longer content to leave his dirty work in the hands of private investigators and canine kidnappers. The enemy had come for Luthor personally.

She watched as he peered in at the tranquilized dog in the cab of the truck, smiling with smug satisfaction.

If you look up "creep" in the dictionary, you'll find a picture of S. Wendell Palomino.

"Nice work, Hiller. Come out and give me a hand!"

The man with the cane emerged from the little house and limped over to the truck. They exchanged a greeting, but there were no friendly handshakes. It was obvious that theirs was strictly a business relationship.

With great effort, the two men unloaded Luthor's inert form and carried it over to be placed in the hatchback of the SUV. The sight of them—one hobbled and limping, and the other short, pudgy, and out of shape—struggling along with a hundred and fifty pounds of deadweight would have been funny if it hadn't been so awful. Hiller had handled the dog better by himself.

Swindle shut the lift gate. "Stupid mutt sure doesn't look like Best in Show now." He emitted a nasty laugh at his own joke.

Hiller didn't share his amusement. "You've got some money for me?"

Swindle nodded. "Let's get out of this rain." They headed into the cottage and shut the door behind them.

Without leaving the bushes, Pitch crept over to a window and peeked inside. She could see Swindle at the kitchen table, peeling bills off a thick roll, while Hiller watched over his shoulder.

The fact that they had loaded Luthor straight into the rental rather than bringing him inside the cabin worried her. That meant their stay here would probably be brief. Once Swindle drove off with the dog, their chances of ever finding him again would be zero—he could be going straight from here to the airport, and off to California. All Griffin's planning and Savannah's dog-whispering couldn't reach the Doberman from a distance of three thousand miles. What would happen next came straight from everyone's wildest nightmares: Luthor would be used for his earning power and then thrown away. And Swindle would put his newfound wealth to work exacting revenge on the kids he believed had ruined his life.

With the two men occupied, she scampered over to the SUV, popped the hatch, and leaned close to a clipped ear. "Wake up, buddy!" She cupped her hands together, allowing the basket of her palms to fill up with rain. Then she dumped the water over his head and snout. "Nap time's over. Let's go." She repeated the action—cup, fill, dump; cup, fill, dump. Luthor didn't even flinch. Her one satisfaction was that Swindle's car now smelled like wet dog. She had managed to splash everything in the back, which was not much — an ice scraper with the logo of the rental company, several empty snack bags and wrappers, and a frayed and finger-marked file folder with a sheaf of crinkled papers protruding from it.

Her eyes fell on the exposed letterhead of the top page:

DISTRICT COURT
STATE OF NEW YORK, COUNTY OF NASSAU
CEDARVILLE DIVISION

Court papers! This was a file about Luthor!

Breathlessly, she opened the folder, and found herself looking at Judge Bittner's order for the Drysdales to hand over the Doberman pinscher known as Luthor. The next item was a packet from a company called Pedigree Research, L.L.C. It was hard to follow, but it seemed to be Luthor's family tree, going back dozens of generations. Apparently, Luthor could be traced all the way back to 1890, when Karl Louis Freidrich Dobermann developed the breed.

"Dude, you're an aristocrat," she murmured to the slumbering dog.

She skipped down to a section in boldface type at the bottom of the fourth page under the heading SPECIAL NOTE:

Here we see a classic example of the so-called "Koenig Doberman," an oversized yet perfectly pure version of the breed first noted in the Schwabian Alps in the early 1950s. Although it was believed at the time that the Koenigs had been interbred with Great Dane bloodlines, this has been proven false. It is now regarded as a naturally occurring phenomenon. Today, the Koenig Doberman is extremely rare. Luthor may be the only purebred example in the United States . . .

"No wonder Swindle wants you," Pitch whispered. "You're probably worth a fortune."

She turned to the very back of the file, and there it was. She might have passed over it, since it was much less official-looking than the other papers in the file. The words *Cedarville Dog Pound* had been scribbled in ballpoint pen at the top of a generic form. It attested to the fact that S. Wendell Palomino was hereby relinquishing his ownership of the Doberman Luthor to the care of the Cedarville Pound, and that he would not be reclaiming him. Swindle's signature was unmistakable at the bottom of the page.

The expression on Pitch's face was something close to unholy glee. "Gotcha," she whispered, folding the paper in quarters and cramming it in the cargo pocket of her climbing shorts. This was the missing document that proved beyond a shadow of a doubt that Luthor belonged to the Drysdales. When he saw this, Judge Bittner would reverse his court order in a heartbeat, and Savannah's long nightmare would be over.

Pitch frowned. Judge Bittner wasn't here. And when Swindle took off with Luthor, who was right and who was wrong wouldn't matter anymore. Even if Savannah showed this document to the judge, he might have no power at all over a dog that had been taken to California.

Pitch wanted to howl her frustration to the four winds. To have the solution to everything but no way to put it into action created an anger that almost generated heat. But what could she do? She couldn't wake the dog up, and she couldn't carry him away. She had no idea where she was, and no phone to communicate with the rest of the team or the outside world.

She set her jaw. She was a climber, and climbers learned to rely on themselves for everything because they couldn't always count on somebody else being there to come to the rescue. She shouldn't need anybody else. She should be able to do this all by herself.

Too bad she couldn't just get in the car and step on the gas. Wouldn't that be something—for Swindle to look out the window and see his SUV, his Koenig Doberman, and his future plans for wealth and revenge disappearing down the road.

When the answer came to her, it was so simple that it brought a smile to her lips. Maybe *she* couldn't drive, but she could also fix it so that no one else could, either.

With a glance at the house to confirm that the coast was still clear, she snuck to the driver's door, reached under the dashboard, and popped the hood. Then she came around to the front and peered in at the engine. How did you disable a car? Melissa probably knew, but she was miles away at Ta-da!

Pitch unclipped her climbing knife. Since the car was off, there would be no electricity in the wires. She cut every cable and connection she could see. If that didn't shut down the SUV, nothing would. Gently, she eased the hood closed, and did the same to the engine of the pickup. Then she returned to the security of the bushes. She was wet, tired, lost, and helpless, yet exhilaration rushed through her like the power from a backup generator.

She couldn't wait until these two clowns tried to start their cars.

If Ben wasn't too thrilled with this adventure, Ferret Face was in open revolt.

The little creature peered out from Ben's collar and hissed vigorously, partly protected from the downpour by his master's chin. Ben knew from experience that this was a sign of ferret displeasure. But never before had he heard the sound so loud, so bitter, and for so long a time, as on this bike ride.

"Cut it out, Ferret Face. I *get* it," he mumbled, hunched over the handlebars into the wind and rain. "You think this is my idea of a fun day?"

He felt as if he'd been riding forever, although that might have been the sheer misery of the weather. He was as wet as if he'd jumped in a pool with all his clothes on. His shorts felt like they'd been permanently epoxied to the banana seat. His thighs had chafed through all three layers of skin. His leg muscles were in agony, and his neck had stiffened to the point of locking completely. That last symptom was fine with Ben.

If he turned his head, he might lose his laser-straight focus on the tire track of the pickup. The only thing worse than enduring this torture was doing it for nothing—making a wrong turn and winding up lost as well as drenched, exhausted, in big trouble for disappearing from camp, and dealing with a mutinous ferret.

Ben hadn't been thrilled when Ebony Lake had refused to take Ferret Face. Still, he figured there was one advantage to going to a different summer camp than Griffin: No way would he get mixed up in another one of his best friend's plans. Yet here he was, miles from Endless Pines, drenched and half-dead, pedaling his guts out for Operation Hideout. He couldn't lose Luthor—and he was becoming even more concerned about Pitch. She still hadn't called. Either that or his phone had become so waterlogged in his pocket that it was no longer working. Anything was possible in this monsoon.

He had been traveling in the same muddy tire rut for so long that when he finally bounced out of it, he nearly lost control of the bike, wheeling around in a panic.

What happened to the tracks? Why did they stop?

Then he realized that the tracks *didn't* stop. They pulled off the road onto the property of a small cottage. And there was the pickup—a red crew cab parked next to a small SUV.

Ferret Face angled his long nose around Ben's chin to peer up at him hopefully.

"This is the place," Ben confirmed.

His momentary triumph at having tracked down the vehicle that had made off with the Doberman was soon replaced by an overpowering icy dread. Luthor's kidnapper was a professional criminal working for Swindle — a sleazy, ruthless moneygrubber determined to exploit the poor dog and then come back to ruin all their lives. Ben had to assume that the driver of the other car wasn't exactly the Tooth Fairy, either. So he couldn't just knock on the door and demand Luthor in the name of truth, justice, and the American way. In fact, it wasn't a really smart idea to let the occupants of the cottage know he was even here.

He stashed the bike in the roadside ditch, where it looked like it belonged. The stealthiest approach to the house seemed to be a line of bushes that passed by a front window. If he could see inside, he might have a better idea of what he was up against. Then he could call Griffin at Ebony Lake and ask what his next move should be.

He ducked into the thick shrubbery and began to inch his way on all fours toward the house. The mud was unimaginable, and the scratchy brambles forced Ferret Face to take refuge under Ben's left arm, where he clung for dear life, claws digging into the soft flesh.

Ben was making steady, if painful, progress, when suddenly a human forearm appeared out of the leafy wetness and slammed into his jaw. He saw stars. A second strike came from the right — an open-handed slap to the ear. This time the stars had streamers. Next it was a heavy boot coming his way. He dodged before it took his head off, but his roll flushed Ferret Face out of his hiding place. The little fellow fell to the dirt, landing on all fours, back arched, teeth bared, ready to fight for his master.

A gasp of shock came from the attacker. *"Ferret Face?"*

Ben was even more surprised. "Pitch? What are you doing here?"

"Some guy grabbed Luthor out of the tower," she whispered. "I couldn't let him get away, so I jumped in the payload of his truck. How did you find us?"

"It's a long story," Ben admitted. "Turns out Ferret Face likes steak. And before I knew it, I was on a bike following your tire tracks."

"A bike?" she echoed. "Ben, that's awesome! Now we've got a way to get out of here!"

Ben was incredulous. "Luthor can ride a bike?"

"Luthor's been tranquilized," Pitch told him. "He's out cold in the back of that SUV. And you know whose rental it is? Swindle's!"

"He came himself this time?"

Pitch nodded. "I guess he got sick of hiring people who kept messing up."

Ben looked haunted. "The amount that guy hates us gives me the creeps. I mean, I hate him, too, but I'm not basing the rest of my life on it."

"Don't obsess about it," Pitch advised in a no-nonsense tone. "We have to act fast. If they loaded Luthor straight into the SUV, it means they're planning on leaving pretty soon."

"But what can we do?" Ben protested. "The bike's barely rideable. Who knows if it'll take two of us? And definitely not two of us carrying a ten-ton dog."

"No, no, no. We'll drape him over the seat and walk him out of here."

Ben looked worried. "We won't get very far. They've got cars."

Pitch could not hold back a diabolical grin. "Well, they have and they haven't. I mean, the cars are here, but they probably won't start." She reached into her pocket and showed him a fistful of multicolored wires, torn and broken, some contacts still attached. "I made a few minor adjustments."

He regarded her in awe. "You've got more guts than brains. But you've got to know that we can't wheel him all the way back to camp."

"We don't have to," she argued. "We just have to get him away from Swindle. Listen—I found something important in the SUV. Remember that missing form from the Cedarville Pound? It proves that Swindle gave Luthor up, which means the Drysdales adopted him fair and square. Well, I've got it right here." She patted her pocket.

Ben brightened. "That's fantastic! Here's my

phone—let's call the police, and all this can be over."

Pitch shook her head. "Swindle still has the court order, and that carries the most weight until it's overturned. Cops aren't judges; they'd just give the dog to Swindle until Bittner rules on the new evidence. By that time, Swindle could take Luthor to California and disappear. Even if the Drysdales win, it'll take years—and tons of money on legal fees—to get a Long Island court ruling enforced on the other side of the country."

"How unfair is that?" Ben complained. "It was bad enough when Swindle had the law on his side. But now *we* have the law on *our* side, and we're no better off!"

Pitch shrugged. "As long as we've got Luthor, we're still in this fight."

Giving the cottage's front window a wide berth, the two retrieved Ben's bike from the ditch and leaned it against the SUV.

"Where'd you get this thing?" Pitch remarked, taking in the ancient rusted frame, now even muddier than before. "The Smithsonian?"

"We're using it for dog transportation, not to enter into the Tour de France," Ben retorted. "Be grateful for the banana seat. That's a little extra room for Luthor."

Deciding to move a huge, unconscious Doberman and actually doing it were two very different matters. A hundred fifty pounds was a lot of weight for any two kids to carry; to have it disproportionately spread throughout the rippled musculature of a large canine body made it nearly impossible. Eventually, the stronger and more athletic Pitch got underneath the heavier head, shoulders, and front legs, leaving Ben to contend with the hindquarters.

As the dog was lifted free of the hatch, Ferret Face emerged from Ben's sleeve, scampered out onto Luthor's back, and made himself comfortable in the short black fur.

"Come back!" Ben hissed. As light as the ferret was, adding any extra mass to Luthor's load was unacceptable.

Now came the hard part—fitting all that bulk on the bicycle. They approached from several different angles, but each seemed to leave the Doberman hanging in a precarious way. They finally draped Luthor's hind legs over the Mustang handlebars, placing his chest and great head on the banana seat.

"We're not going to get it any better than this," Pitch panted. "Now, let's blow this Popsicle stand before Swindle and his goon decide to check on Luthor."

Pitch got on one side, Ben got on the other, and they started slowly down the road. The bike carried Luthor's weight easily. But in order to maintain balance, the two rescuers had to lean into each other, which made progress exhausting.

"How long do we have to keep this up?" Ben gasped.

Pitch's reply was strained. "As long as it takes."

36

Dominic Hiller pocketed his money and stood up, leaning heavily on his cane. "I wish I could say it was a pleasure doing business with you, Mr. Palomino. But I've got one torn-up knee that says it wasn't."

Swindle glowered at him. "Excuse me for thinking you and your friend knew how to handle yourselves around a couple of kids."

"Those aren't ordinary kids," Hiller defended himself. "Their loyalty to that dumb animal is insane. It's almost like a cult. It leads them to perform miracles."

"Yeah, well, they just ran out of miracles," Palomino retorted sourly. "I've got the dog, and within a week, every top breeder in the world will be watching him wipe up the competition on the show circuit. That 'dumb animal' is going to make me rich."

"We should have hit you up for more money," Hiller mused, limping toward the door. "Especially Louie. He's got whiplash from when the bug dipper came down on him."

They left the cottage and started for their two vehicles.

The first yelp came from Palomino. "The dog's escaped!"

"No chance! He's out cold for hours yet!"

"Then how do you explain *this*?" Swindle roared.

Hiller thumped over to see for himself. Sure enough, the SUV's hatchback was empty.

"I can't!" The hired man was mystified. "Even if he woke up early, how would he get himself out of the car? He doesn't have fingers, you know."

"Which means he had help!" Palomino growled. "Those kids must have followed us somehow."

"They can't have gone far," Hiller reasoned. "You drive north, I'll drive south. We'll catch them."

Distraught, Swindle leaped into his rental SUV, jammed the key into the ignition, and twisted it. The car did not start. He tried again. Nothing. Not a cough, not a rev, not even a hiccup.

"Cheap rental piece of junk!" He leaped out and ran to Hiller's truck. "My car won't start!"

"*Your* car won't start!" Hiller was pounding on the steering wheel. "Mine won't, either!"

They raced around and threw open the hood. Cut and tattered wires were everywhere. On the SUV, the situation was the same.

Sabotage.

"Those kids!" Hiller exclaimed in agony. "Is there anything they can't do?"

Palomino was upset, but not rattled. "We can still catch them."

"How?"

"On foot."

Hiller waved his cane. "I'm not exactly an Olympic athlete these days."

"They're still kids, and they're carrying a ton of dog meat." The fried-egg eyes grew even wider behind the Coke-bottle glasses as Swindle looked down into the mud of the road. There, the track of a single wheel, much narrower than a car tire, led off to the south.

Hiller followed his gaze. "A wheelbarrow?"

"Whatever it is, they're probably just around the bend. Let's go."

They started off down the road, with the out-of-shape former storekeeper barely keeping ahead of his hobbled hired man. Soon they were soaked and mud to the knees.

"Lousy kids!" Swindle puffed. "Lousy kids!" After the first quarter mile, he had no breath left for any words at all.

Hiller's cane kept sticking in the soft ground, and he took to limping along without leaning on it, waving it in front of him like a sword.

At last, they rounded a curve in the road, and their quarry appeared out of the mist and rain.

Palomino pointed. "There. Three of them."

Hiller's eyesight was sharper. "Just two. That's the dog in the middle. They've got him draped over a bike."

The two men quickened their pace, hoping the poor weather would cover their approach. It worked for a while. But then one of the kids—the girl—happened to glance over her shoulder.

The first Ben knew of it, Pitch had accelerated her pace, and he had to jog to keep up with the bike. "Hey, what are you—?"

"Run, Ben!" she interrupted urgently. "Swindle's after us!"

Terrified, Ben looked back at the two lumbering pursuers. The men were slow, but the overladen bicycle was slower. "Let's move!" he urged.

They pushed with all their might, which only seemed to dig the bike's wheels deeper into the mud.

Pitch's face was a picture of determination. "Faster!" she breathed.

Sweat ran down their faces, mingling with the rain. Gradually, the bicycle picked up momentum. The gap between them and the two men, which had been closing steadily, began to open up again.

Then it happened. The front tire hit an exposed root and bounced. With it bounced Luthor, down to the ground, where he rolled into the ditch. Pitch and Ben dropped the bike and stooped to lift him out, but it was impossible to get any leverage on so much weight.

"Come on, Luthor, wake up," Pitch pleaded with the slumbering dog. "You can nap all you want once we get away, but right now we have to *go*!"

Too late. Swindle and Hiller appeared at the top of the ditch, panting and glaring down at them. "Fancy meeting you kids here," drawled S. Wendell Palomino in an unpleasant, if breathless tone.

Ferret Face shrank inside Ben's collar. Even the little animal could see the hopelessness of their situation. Luthor was still immobile, and the enemy was upon them.

This was the end of the road.

All at once, Pitch sprang away from the Doberman, grabbed Ben's hand, and hauled him out of the ditch. They pounded through the wet underbrush, making for the cover of the trees. Hiller started to chase them, but came down too hard on his injured leg and hit the ground with a splash beside Luthor. By the time he'd gotten back up again, Pitch and Ben were disappearing into the woods.

He started after them in pursuit.

"Forget it," Palomino told him. "We've got the mutt. That's all that matters."

"They could go to the cops!" Hiller sputtered.

"And tell them what?" Swindle challenged. "That we stopped them from stealing *my* dog? We've got the law on our side. Now we just need a mechanic to fix the cars, and we'll never have to deal with those rotten kids again."

At least not until I'm ready to go back to Cedarville and take them all down. Palomino thought it, but he didn't say it aloud.

It wasn't easy for slight Ben to keep up with Pitch's long athletic strides, but he came close, sprinting through the forest, sidestepping trees like a broken-field runner in a football game. When at last he drew close enough to reach out and grab a fistful of her T-shirt, he nearly pulled her over backward.

She paused for a moment, listening for footsteps crashing through the woods behind them. "I think we're safe."

Ben collapsed to his knees, hyperventilating. "Why did we do that? Why did we run?" he rasped. "We abandoned Luthor!"

"We didn't abandon him," Pitch corrected firmly. "We lived on to fight another day."

"Try telling that to Savannah!" Ben croaked. "Try telling it to Griffin! The whole point of the plan is keeping Luthor away from Swindle. We just did the total opposite of that!"

"Cool your jets," Pitch soothed. "They've got the dog, but they're not going anywhere anytime soon."

"And we are?" Ben challenged. "We don't even have a way to get back to camp."

"Never mind camp," she told him. "Give me your phone. It's time to call in the troops."

37

The score was 3–2, with a man on third, when Griffin's stomach began vibrating.

Crouched behind home plate in his catcher's mask and chest protector, he had no way of answering the phone that was taped to his belly. Cyrus had already confiscated Savannah's cell—the girl was so frantic over what might be happening to Luthor that she was constantly being caught using it at unauthorized times. If Griffin lost his phone, too, they'd be completely out of touch with the plan.

But he had to take this call. It could only be about Operation Hideout.

The vibration stopped.

Oh, no! I missed it! Call back! Please call back!

The batter hit a weak dribbler out toward the mound. It was the pitcher's play, but at that moment, the phone began to vibrate once more. Griffin charged the ball as if he'd been shot out of a cannon. He flattened the pitcher as the boy bent to field the grounder, scooped up the ball himself, and made a bee-line for the base path. Spying the danger, the runner reversed course and headed back to third. He should have been caught in a rundown except that Griffin had no time to waste on baseball. He had to make the out and scram in time to answer his call.

With a burst of speed that surprised even him, Griffin executed the tag, shouted, *"Bathroom break!"* and sprinted for the wash station, jettisoning equipment as he fled.

"What?" he panted when he was finally able to rip the phone from his skin and hit TALK.

"Swindle's got Luthor and we're lost in the woods!" Ben babbled on the other end of the line.

It was the last thing any planner wanted to hear—that the wheels were coming off and there was nothing to be done about it.

"Calm down," Griffin ordered. "Tell me what's going on."

"We're not lost," came Pitch's voice.

"We just don't know where we are!" Ben added helpfully.

"We know exactly where Luthor is—that's the main thing," Pitch explained. "Swindle's got him tranquilized in a cabin maybe a quarter mile from here."

"Any idea what the jerk's going to do?" Griffin probed, struggling for calm.

"Well, he's not going to drive away," she replied. "Not until he finds a good mechanic. But there's another guy with him, and there's no way Ben and I can handle both of them without help."

"Sit tight," Griffin ordered tersely. "We'll be there as soon as we can."

Ben was practically hysterical. "How can you find us? *We* can't even find us!"

"Your phone has a GPS. Melissa will know how to locate it. This is going to be a whole team effort."

He hung up, taking note of the clock. Savannah, he knew, was in Arts and Crafts, tie-dyeing T-shirts. The next truck coming by would be the Sewer and Septic Service, also known as the Triple-S. It wasn't Griffin's preferred choice of transportation, but it was the soonest option.

And he had a sinking feeling that time was running out.

Logan finally loved camp—and it was because camp finally loved Logan.

He was getting the respect he deserved at last. After his Showdown-saving performance of Abraham Lincoln being attacked by a dog, he was the number one star at Ta-da! Well, technically, *Melissa* was number one. But since she had given up singing and would only work on set design, that left Logan in the top spot. Better still, Mary Catherine the Klingon was way down at the bottom of the totem pole with the termites.

Case in point: Today's improvisation exercise in the performance center, *Nile Story*. Logan was Pharaoh, and Mary Catherine was the priestess of some minor god nobody cared about. Best of all, this was improv, which meant there was no script, and the actors were making it up as they went along.

"Come to Pharaoh, O random priestess," Logan commanded in an imperious tone. "It is hot, and our royal feet perspire with great foulness unpleasant to our nose. Wash our sandals in the purifying water of the Nile."

Red-faced but obedient, the unfortunate priestess was unlacing his sneakers when Melissa burst into the barn. "Great Pharaoh," she announced, a little out of breath. "Follow me. You are needed on an urgent errand."

"Pharaohs don't do errands," Logan replied haughtily. "That is what servants are for." He regarded Mary Catherine sternly. "To the Nile with haste, priestess. Let not the palace gates strike the rear of thy tunic on the way out."

"But, Great One," Melissa persisted. "This matter involves the—jackal. The *Doberman* jackal," she added meaningfully.

Logan kicked back into his shoes, stomping on Mary Catherine's fingers.

"Hey!"

"Sorry!" Pharaoh blurted. "I—I forgot to lock my pyramid!" He ran for the exit.

Athena stepped forward. "This is about that poor abused dog, isn't it?"

"The farmer's got him back," Melissa confirmed. "He needs our help—now!"

"He didn't look so abused to me," Mary Catherine put in sourly.

Athena ignored her. "Go! We'll cover for you with Wendy."

They jogged across the compound, Logan hopping to tie his sneakers on the way. "What's the emergency?"

"Swindle's got Luthor," Melissa explained. "Griffin and Savannah are coming to pick us up in the Triple-S."

Logan's nose wrinkled. "Not the Triple-S."

"Faster! They could be here any minute."

They made it to the trees without attracting attention, reaching the road just as a cargo van appeared in the distance.

"That's the one," Logan confirmed sadly. "I can smell it from here."

Sure enough, the familiar logo of the Sewer and Septic Service Corporation came into focus. Melissa and Logan stepped back into the cover of the trees.

As the truck rattled along, a rear door opened slightly and an arm reached out. It unlocked a reel on the side of the van, releasing a long hose. The next time the driver glanced at his mirror, he could see fifty feet of rubber tubing snaking behind him, flapping all over the road.

The truck screeched to a halt, and the driver set about restoring the hose, cursing colorfully. Melissa and Logan tensed for action. There would be a handful of seconds while the man walked back to his cab, climbed in, and restarted the engine. That was all the time they were going to get.

"Now!" Melissa whispered.

They were off like the wind, pounding for the rear of the van. As they approached, the cargo doors opened. Griffin and Savannah hauled them aboard and slammed the hatch shut. Just like that, they were moving again.

"You know, this better be important," Logan complained. "I was about to make Mary Catherine feed me grapes."

"I have no idea what you're talking about," Savannah told him harshly. "But poor Luthor is in danger, so, yes, this definitely counts as important."

The Man With The Plan was grim as he took charge. "Operation Hideout is falling apart, you guys. It's my fault, really. If Swindle could find Ebony Lake and Ta-da!, I should have known he would look to our other two team members at the third camp."

"But how do we know where he's holding Luthor?" Logan asked.

Melissa held up her phone. "I'm tracking the GPS locater on Ben's cell." She frowned. "We're moving in the right direction, but the signal's weaker than it was twenty minutes ago. That could mean the unit is running low on power."

The van was built to carry equipment, not passengers, so the ride was rough, especially when they left pavement and began to jounce along dirt road. All eyes were on Melissa's phone, which pinpointed Ben's location. It was unlikely that the Triple-S was headed exactly where they wanted to go. They had to be vigilant, then. When it seemed as if they were as close as they were likely to get, they had to make their move and bail out of the truck. The rest of the way they would travel on foot.

"How far will that be?" asked Savannah worriedly. For her, every minute Luthor was in Swindle's clutches was torture.

Griffin shrugged. "It depends on the route of the Triple-S, and how far off the main road that cottage happens to be."

Melissa sounded nervous behind her hair. "Ben's signal is down to ten percent. Don't people remember to charge their phones?"

"Just you," Logan confirmed. "The rest of us have careers to think about." He stretched, and his flailing elbow flipped a metal switch. The roar of a motor filled the van, followed by a loud hiss of suction. A length of corrugated tubing lashed out, slapping Logan in the cheek. The air filled with dust, starting them all sneezing and choking. A powerful vacuum tugged at their clothes. Melissa's curtain of long stringy hair was pulled away from her face and sucked into the nozzle.

Griffin lunged for the power vac and flicked the switch again. Blessed quiet returned. Melissa's hair reassembled itself in front of her face.

Nobody spoke. Nobody even moved. Had the driver noticed the disturbance? If he caught them, it would mean the end of Operation Hideout.

The van continued to shudder along, shock absorbers protesting loudly.

"That was close," quavered Savannah.

"It's time," said Melissa in a small voice.

"Time for what?" asked Griffin absently. He was so relieved at having survived the mishap with the power vac that he couldn't focus on anything else.

Melissa held her phone in front of him. They had homed in on Ben's signal, and were now veering away slightly. They would never be closer than this.

Like a bus rider getting up to pull the cord for his stop, Griffin opened the rear door a crack, leaned out, and released the hose from its wheel. The four of them waited, poised for flight, as the truck crunched to a halt. But instead of the squeak of the reel rewinding, the back hatch was flung wide, and the driver was glaring in at them.

I knew I heard something—" the man began angrily.

Without thinking, Griffin lunged for the power vac and kicked the switch in the opposite direction. The machine blared to life, blowing out this time. The gale-force wind took the glasses clean off the driver's nose and sent them skittering down the road.

Nobody needed a signal. The four campers blasted out of the truck. They crossed the road and disappeared into the woods. For the first hundred yards, their flight was pure escape. Then Melissa began to adjust their route according to the blip from Ben's cell. When it became clear that the driver wasn't interested in chasing them, they slowed to a walk.

"The signal's going in and out," Melissa observed. "When the phone dies, we'll be flying blind."

The rain was tapering off, but the ground was swampy. Every step pulled at their sneakers, making progress slow and miserable. Onward they forged until, with sinking hearts, all four of them watched the signal on Melissa's screen flicker and wink out.

Savannah was practically hysterical. "How will we ever find Luthor *now*?"

Griffin asserted his leadership. "Going back isn't part of the plan. We're headed in the right direction. We stick to it as best we can."

"We've been sticking to it for the last hour," Logan pointed out. "Who knows if we can even retrace our path to the road to catch another truck back to camp?"

"I don't care about getting back," Savannah insisted. "I only care about Luthor."

"We have to care about all of it," Griffin said firmly. "If we can't stop Swindle right here, right now, he's going to haunt us for the rest of our lives."

They continued to walk, with a little less sureness in their steps. A lot of the hopeful determination had gone out of them.

And then a voice that was low, yet remarkably close, queried, "What's taking them so long? What if they got caught? What if they can't find us?"

Griffin stopped dead, a goofy grin spreading across his face. "I'd know that whine anywhere."

The four of them rushed through a break in the trees into a clearing at the side of a narrow dirt road. There they found a small cottage, two disabled vehicles, and Pitch and Ben, waiting not very patiently.

Due to their dire situation, the reunion was brief and subdued. As soon as Palomino could find transportation, Luthor would be out of reach. It was the worst kind of ticking clock, since, for all they knew, a tow truck could be right around the next bend.

"Maybe that's our opportunity," Griffin mused. "Swindle will go to the garage with his rental, right? That'll leave Luthor alone with only one guy."

Pitch shook her head. "I only pulled out wires. They might not need to go to a garage."

Melissa nodded. "A trained mechanic could fix that on the spot."

"Knocking out the cars was sheer genius," Griffin praised Pitch. "Without that, the plan would be dead in the water."

"It was an amazing ad lib," added Logan, using theatre terminology.

"That's not all," Pitch enthused. From her back pocket she produced the page she had taken from the SUV—the form from the dog pound that proved Palomino had given up his Doberman.

"We can't leave here without Luthor," Savannah said determinedly. "Judge Bittner will *have* to overturn the court order when he sees this."

"But how do we get to Luthor?" Logan asked. "He's locked in the house with two adults."

"Adults have never stopped us before," put in Griffin. "All they are is bigger than us. That doesn't mean much when you've got the right plan."

"It'll be tricky, though," Pitch acknowledged. "Ben and I already made a play for the dog, so Swindle will be on high alert."

"When's Luthor going to wake up?" wondered Ben, absently rubbing his T-shirt to stroke Ferret Face through the fabric. "He could be our secret weapon. That dog could eat two adults as an appetizer and still have room for a full-grown bull elephant."

Savannah glared at him. "Luthor's as gentle as a lamb."

"To *you*," Pitch told her, not unkindly. "No offense, but to the rest of the world, he's an instrument of destruction. I agree that it's a shame to waste him if things get rough dealing with Swindle."

The dog whisperer was adamant. "I won't allow it. He was trained to be vicious before, and it almost tore him apart."

"And now he's devoted his life to tearing everybody else apart," Ben observed.

Savannah reddened. "If he bit somebody, he'd have to be put down!"

"Fighting among ourselves doesn't help rescue the dog," Griffin said quickly. "The truth is, we have no idea what kind of shape Luthor is in — or how closely Swindle and the other guy are watching him. We need a spy operation."

"There's no time," Savannah protested. "A mechanic could already be on his way to fix the cars!"

"All the more reason we have to spy," Griffin argued. "We can't start planning until we know how long we've got to work with."

"How are we supposed to do that?" Logan challenged.

"Stare in through the window and try to read Swindle's lips?"

"If only we could find a way to hear what they're saying in there," Griffin mused.

"Some Man With The Plan you are," Ben said sarcastically. "I can't believe you forgot to pack an electronic listening device in your duffel bag."

"Actually," Melissa spoke up shyly, "I might be able to help out with that."

Everyone stared at her.

"You brought a *bug* to summer camp?" Pitch asked incredulously.

"Well, no, but I was just thinking." Melissa took her phone out of her pocket. "If I call Griffin, and we place my cell inside the cottage somewhere, it should pick up everything that's being said in there."

"I like it," Griffin approved, his eyes alight with the excitement of a plan beginning to take shape. "But how are we going to get your phone into the house?"

Pitch took the handset from Melissa. "That's the easy part."

Ben was wide-eyed. "There's no mail slot or doggie door, and Swindle knows we're around, so there's no way they left a window unlocked. What are you going to do?"

She grinned. "Think Santa Claus."

39

To Pitch, who had conquered mountain peaks, sheer cliffs, and frozen waterfalls, getting to the roof of the single-story cottage was as easy as stepping onto a footstool. From the eaves, she was amused to look down and see her five teammates watching her movements anxiously. She smirked at them and then crossed to the stone chimney. She hoisted herself up and peered inside. Perfect. There was no damper; she could see clear down to the fireplace about fifteen feet below.

She took out Melissa's phone and began to unwind the makeshift twine they had created by removing leaves from the ivy on the side of the cottage. Pitch secured the handset to one end, triple-knotting it. Then she dialed Griffin.

He answered on the first ring. "Ready?"

"Here goes nothing," she replied, and began to pay out the vine.

The unit descended into the gloom of the chimney.

The ivy was surprisingly strong and clung to the case as if it had been designed especially for that purpose.

The handset disappeared in the darkness of the passage. Pitch continued to lower until, suddenly, the glossy screen was clearly visible in the light of the room below. Quickly, she wound up the ivy until the unit was in shadow again. This was as far as they dared go. The last thing they wanted was for Swindle to glance at his fireplace and see a phone dangling there like a worm on a hook.

Pitch looked down off the roof. The others were huddled in the bushes, crowded around Griffin, who had his phone to his ear. Was it working? she wondered. Could they hear anything?

What was going on?

S. Wendell Palomino was in a towering rage. *"Tomorrow morning?"* he barked into his phone in disbelief. "I can't wait till tomorrow morning! I've got a flight to California *tonight*!"

"Sorry, Mr. Palomino," came the voice on the other end of the line, "but that's not going to happen."

"It *has* to happen!" Swindle stormed. "What kind of garage are you running?"

"This isn't like the big-city outfits you're probably used to. I'm a small operation. It's just me and my truck, and we cover a lot of territory. As you've probably noticed, wet weather means a lot of mud around here. When people start getting stuck, it's first come, first served."

"And you just leave people stranded," Palomino seethed.

"Well, that's another story entirely. Are you telling me you're stranded?"

"Not only am I stranded, I'm exposed to animal attack!" Okay, that was an exaggeration, but Luthor was going to be none too happy when the tranquilizer wore off. "And I've got no way to get my poor injured friend the medical attention he needs."

"Sounds serious," the mechanic agreed.

"Exactly! So how soon can you be here?"

"*I* can't make it till tomorrow, but if things are as bad as you say, you'd better call the police."

"I wouldn't *need* the police if I had a *car*!" Swindle insisted.

"Like I said, I'll be there tomorrow. You don't have to wait around. Stick with your buddy. Just leave the cars unlocked and the keys on the seat. I'll call you as soon as I know what's what."

"Oh, fine," Palomino groaned. "We'll wait for you."

"Are you sure that's wise for your friend?"

"Positive," Swindle replied with a sigh. "In fact, I think he's getting better. Come as soon as you can." He hung up the phone and slumped in his chair. Nothing was ever easy where those lousy kids were involved.

Hiller thumped over on his crutch. "Maybe we

should be calling the police. If our cars have been vandalized, that's a crime."

Palomino shook his head. "The last thing we need is some cop snooping around."

Hiller's eyes narrowed. "You said the dog is legally yours."

"Of course. But the mutt's been tranquilized, which is going to seem fishy to some small-town flatfoot. If he gets a sniff that there are kids involved—runaways, no less—that's a can of worms I don't want to open." Swindle surveyed the kitchen irritably. "Is there anything to eat in this dump?"

The hired man limped for the door. "I've got a turkey sandwich out in the truck. Tell you what: I'll split it with you if you promise me we're the good guys."

Palomino grimaced. "Do I look like a crook to you?"

Griffin's face suddenly went white, and he waved the phone up at Pitch on the roof, gesturing wildly. She shot him a questioning shrug, but by then, he and the other team members had ducked out of sight in the bushes.

The sound she heard next made her stiffen in fear: the opening and closing of the cottage's front door.

Hiller stepped out of the house and started for the pickup truck.

If he looks over his shoulder, he'll be staring straight at me!

Her nerveless fingers lost their grip on the vine, and Melissa's phone was falling. Fumbling madly, she caught the line, stopping the unit three inches from shattering against the base of the fireplace. Heart pounding, she dove for the apex of the A-frame roof. If she could make it over the top before Swindle's man turned around . . .

As she somersaulted over the peak, a horrible realization came to her: She had misjudged the slope. Down the other side she skidded, tumbling out of control.

40

Mustering all her strength and climbing skill, Pitch wedged the heel of her sneaker against a kitchen vent. Her momentum spun her upside down, sliding toward the edge. At the last second, she reached above her head, locked a pincer grip on the eaves, and squeezed. Her motion shuddered to a stop. She hung there, her hair cascading off the roof. Out of the corner of her eye, she could see Griffin and the team crouched in the foliage, staring up at her in horror. Another second or two and she would have gone over the side.

Oblivious to the drama unfolding above him, Hiller got a small paper bag out of the pickup and went back inside the house. The crisis had ended as quickly as it had begun.

Gingerly, Pitch got herself turned around and made her way back to the chimney. Winding the vine around her arm like the spool of a fishing rod, she reeled the phone out of the flue. Then she shinnied down the drainpipe and rejoined her friends.

Even Ferret Face regarded her in awe.

"Are you okay?" Ben hissed. "Man, I figured we'd be scraping you out of the weeds with a spatula!"

"First rule of climbing," Pitch told him bravely. "If it didn't happen, there's no point in stressing over it."

"The important thing is we got the information we needed," The Man With The Plan reminded everybody. "Swindle and the other jerk are stuck until morning. Which means we've got some time to make our move on Luthor."

"We haven't got *that* much time," Ben put in. "Pitch and I have been AWOL from camp since this morning. If we don't get back soon, the counselors are going to start to panic."

"We can't worry about any of that," Savannah insisted. "The only thing that matters is saving Luthor."

"That's another problem," Pitch pointed out. "The dog weighs a ton. We can lift him—but not with two people chasing us. Been there, done that."

Melissa had a suggestion. "Maybe we can wait till they go to sleep."

Griffin nodded. "The question is how do we get in the house?"

"The roof won't work," Pitch supplied. "No way into the attic, no skylight."

"An unlocked window?" asked Logan.

Griffin shook his head. "We can't depend on it. Besides, the house is so small, we could be climbing straight into Swindle's lap."

Stealthily, Griffin approached the little cabin, the others trailing behind him. Crouched in the cover of the bushes, they circled the outside. Griffin stopped in front of a pair of flat, wooden cellar doors, separate from the house.

Pitch indicated the heavy padlock that barred the entryway. "How are you going to get through *that*?"

Griffin knelt on the damp ground to investigate. The lock was metal, but the doors themselves were ancient wood, softened by decades of northeastern weather. He began to work with his thumbs, trying to create some separation between the iron hasp and the rotted panel. "Quick—see if you can find something to jam under here."

Melissa handed over a sharp wedge-shaped rock. "Try this."

Griffin inserted the pointed edge beneath the cleat and pressed down, levering the hasp away from the door. With light popping sounds, the softened wood gave way, and the cleat came off in his hand, still attached to the lock. Slowly, he opened the doors, trying to minimize the squeaking of the ancient rusted hinges. The gust of air that came up to greet them was musty and coolly damp. They squinted into the gloom of a root cellar, with stone walls and a dirt floor.

"Yuck," said Logan. "There could be mice down there."

"And don't you dare disturb any of them," Savannah told him. "They're animals, just like the rest of us."

Ben looked down his own collar. "Hear that, Ferret Face? No hunting."

"Keep him safe inside your shirt," Griffin ordered. "The last thing we need is you falling asleep in hostile territory."

Melissa called up the flashlight app on her phone and handed it to Griffin. He led the way down the six steps into the cavelike cellar. The cobwebs were so thick that progress was like passing through lace curtains. Savannah gagged.

"What's the matter?" Pitch whispered. "Aren't spiders animals just like the rest of us?"

The space was empty save for a few potato sacks and a broken bushel basket. The toe of Melissa's sneaker nudged an ancient potato, only to have it crumble to dust.

"When's the last time anybody came down here?" hissed Ben in revulsion.

"They forgot about this place when they started remembering the Alamo," Pitch replied in a low voice.

Griffin held out his arms beside him. The group halted and fell silent. They had reached another staircase, this one leading to a small door. Light was visible around the edges. It was the entrance to the house. Muffled conversation wafted through the door—Swindle and his man.

The enemy was no more than a few yards away.

"What now?" Savannah barely whispered.

"We chill," Griffin informed them.

"Here?" quavered Logan, plucking a shred of cobweb from the end of his nose. "The Screen Actors Guild would never approve these conditions!"

"Ferret Face doesn't like the dark," Ben warned.

"Don't be stupid," Savannah said sharply. "Ferrets are most active at murky times like dawn or dusk. They're crepuscular."

"Yeah, but I'm not!" Ben complained.

"We have to be able to tell when Swindle and the other guy go to sleep," Griffin explained. "As soon as it gets quiet on the other side of the door, that's when we make our move."

"Let's switch our phones to airplane mode to save battery life," Melissa advised. "Once the sun goes down, they'll be the only light we've got."

41

Mr. Bing was rewiring a SmartPick™ that had short circuited.

He tightened the connections, replaced the cover, and pressed the button. With a whirring sound, the titanium fruit-picking pole telescoped across the kitchen, poking his wife in the small of the back.

Mrs. Bing let out a yelp, juggling and nearly dropping a heavy casserole dish. She turned on her husband. "Why don't you take that thing to your workshop before you put it through a wall?"

"It's so empty around here with Griffin away at camp," the inventor complained. "Who would have thought one kid could fill up a whole house?"

"Well, he *is* The Man With The Plan," she reminded him.

He grinned. "Not at Ebony Lake, he isn't. That's the best thing about sending him to the back of beyond—none of his scheming. Not unless he's organizing a woodchuck insurrection."

"I know what you mean," Mrs. Bing agreed a little guiltily. "I guess I never admitted to myself how nerve-racking it is to be Griffin's mother."

Ri-i-i-ing!

Mr. Bing set down his invention and answered the phone. "Hello . . . speaking . . ."

The receiver slipped from his hand and hit the floor with a clatter. He stooped to fumble it back to his lips. "Are you absolutely sure?"

"What is it?" his wife asked anxiously.

Mr. Bing held up a finger. "Right—we'll be there as soon as we can." He hung up and dialed Griffin's cell. The call went straight to voicemail.

"What's going on?" Mrs. Bing demanded.

Her husband's face was gray. "Griffin's disappeared."

"What do you mean, 'disappeared'?"

"He and one other camper never came to the mess hall for dinner. No one's seen them for at least a few hours."

They were in the car, heading north, inside of three minutes.

Waiting in line to pay the toll at the Throgs Neck Bridge, Mrs. Bing frowned as a familiar SUV roared past in the E-ZPass lane. "Wasn't that Rick Drysdale's car?"

"With Griffin missing, I hardly think that's our number one priority right now."

"Griffin's missing *along with one other camper,*" she persisted. "Isn't Savannah at Ebony Lake, too?"

When the phone rang inside the SUV, Mr. Drysdale had no time for a conversation. "Sorry, can't talk now. We're heading up to Ebony Lake. Savannah's gone missing."

"So has Griffin," Mrs. Bing told him. "How much do you want to bet that, wherever they are, they're together?"

A quarter mile farther on, the Bings' van pulled alongside the stopped SUV on the shoulder. Mrs. Bing and Mr. Drysdale rolled down their windows.

"What do you think the kids have gotten themselves into this time?" Mrs. Drysdale called anxiously.

Mrs. Bing didn't answer. She was staring at a sedan that had just sped past them on the highway. "Wasn't that Pete and Estelle Slovak?"

It took a moment for the significance of that statement to sink in.

"How could Ben be with Savannah and Griffin?" Mr. Drysdale asked. "He went to a different camp entirely."

Griffin's mother was already dialing her phone. "There's one way to find out." And when Mrs. Slovak's voice came on the line, she asked, "Estelle—is everything all right with Ben?"

Ben's mother sounded distraught. "Endless Pines just called. Nobody's seen Benjamin since—" Sudden silence on the line. "How could you know something's wrong?"

"Griffin and Savannah Drysdale have vanished from Ebony Lake."

Mrs. Slovak was amazed. "And you think they're with my Benjamin? These camps are scattered across the north woods, with no transportation at all! That's impossible."

"One thing I've learned from Griffin is that *nothing* is impossible," Mrs. Bing said in a determined tone.

"I'm going to call the Benson girl's family," Mrs. Slovak decided. "She was at camp with Benjamin. Maybe they've heard something from her."

When Mrs. Slovak finally reached Pitch's father, she made an alarming discovery: Pitch's parents were at a rest area on the New York State Thruway about ten miles ahead. While stopped to ask directions to Camp Endless Pines, they had spotted the Kellermans' car at the gas pump. And in the Kellermans' backseat were none other than Mr. and Mrs. Dukakis.

"Are you saying that Antonia, Logan, and Melissa all disappeared from their camps today?" Ben's mother cried.

Mr. Benson was stunned. "How did you know?"

Mrs. Slovak was hyperventilating as she gasped out the details of the missing Griffin, Savannah, and Ben.

Six campers AWOL. Six Cedarville friends. Six members of Griffin's team.

This was no coincidence. There was only one thing it could possibly be.

A plan.

42

The two parent parades sped north on the Thruway, connected via cell phone conference call. At a fuel stop, all five vehicles met up, and the two groups merged into one. The procession from Cedarville exited the highway a little farther on, heading west on a two-lane rural route. A half mile from the interchange, the streetlights ended, and they navigated without GPS in the darkness. To the residents of the farms they passed, they must have seemed like a funeral cortege, a tight formation of cars on otherwise deserted roads.

As they approached the vicinity of the three camps, the parents faced a dilemma: Unlike their children, they were planless. Should they split up, with the Bings and Drysdales proceeding to Ebony Lake, the Dukakises and Kellermans to Ta-da!, and the Slovaks and Bensons to Endless Pines? That made sense, except that everyone was convinced that the six missing friends were together. Perhaps they should remain en masse and visit the camps one at a time, maintaining a united front.

"Why go to the camps at all?" Mrs. Slovak challenged. "Those are the only places we know for sure that our children *aren't*."

Mr. Bing had a suggestion. "Let's stop at a diner and talk this out over coffee. We've all been on the road for three hours. We're not thinking straight."

"Good idea," approved Mr. Kellerman, three cars back. "Is there any place open around here?"

Towns were few and far between in these woods. The biggest businesses were the summer camps, and they provided their own food service. Mile after mile of wooded nothingness unspooled before the parent parade.

Just as Mr. Bing was about to despair, a neon sign flickered up on the left.

FOO   T
GAR G   EL

"Foot gargle?" his wife repeated, bewildered.

But as they drew closer, they could see that the glowing letters had burned out over the years. Illuminated by headlights, the message was:

FOOD GIFTS
GARAGE FUEL

The place turned out to be a grimy gas station that sold drinks, snacks, and cheap souvenirs from a row of dilapidated vending machines. The twelve parents sat down over watery coffee to weigh their options.

Mrs. Slovak was becoming visibly more agitated every minute. "Why aren't they answering their phones?"

"Maybe they don't have them," Mrs. Bing suggested. "The rule at Ebony Lake is to leave all devices powered off in the cabins. Besides messages home, they're supposed to be just for emergencies."

"*This* isn't an emergency?" Mrs. Slovak demanded.

"The reception is probably spotty out in the sticks," suggested Mr. Kellerman.

"Or their batteries are dead," added Mrs. Dukakis. "Melissa is always running dozens of applications. What for is beyond me, but I do know that power drain is a problem."

"Let's focus on the big picture," Mr. Bing advised. "Out in the wilderness, separated by not just miles but entire forests, our kids have managed to get themselves in some kind of trouble."

"Trouble!" Ben's mother spat. "Why don't you call it by its real name? It's your son who's The Man With The Plan!"

"But what kind of plan could they possibly have around here?" wondered Mrs. Benson.

And then an all-too-familiar name was spoken in the tiny shop: *Palomino.*

Two men leaned on the counter. One, in greasy coveralls, was chewing on a cinnamon bun and talking with his mouth full. "Guy called himself Palomino. Real obnoxious. Must be from downstate."

Mr. Drysdale stood up. "Excuse me, are you talking about S. Wendell Palomino?"

"Didn't catch the fellow's first name," the mechanic replied. "He a friend of yours?"

Savannah's father flushed. "In a manner of speaking."

"Well, you might want to take a ride over to the old Peterson place, seeing as how I can't get there till morning."

Mrs. Slovak spoke up. "Did he mention anything about children? Thirteen-year-olds?"

The coveralled man shook his head. "Nah, nothing about any kids. Says he's got a friend who needs a doctor, but he was just angling to jump the line and get his car fixed ahead of schedule. Says a lot of things, this character, none of them too pleasant."

"It can't be a coincidence," Mr. Bing whispered. "Palomino? Near the three camps? Not too pleasant?"

"You don't think he'd hurt the kids, do you?" Mrs. Kellerman asked anxiously.

"This could be about Luthor," Mr. Drysdale mused. "Maybe he hid the dog so he can sue us for stealing him."

"Where is this Peterson place?" Mr. Bing called to the mechanic.

"Head west about thirty miles," the man replied. "Left turn on the dirt road. You can't miss it. It's the only house around."

43

Once night had fallen, the root cellar of the old cottage was smothered in suffocating darkness. The phones provided occasional light for a while. But as the minutes ticked into hours, and batteries dwindled and died, these intervals became a luxury the team could no longer afford. Soon only Melissa's handset had any life at all, thanks to a few power-saving improvements the brilliant girl had invented. And even she dared not use her flashlight app for fear of squandering what little juice she had left.

"Don't these people ever sleep?" Ben complained in a peeved whisper.

"Big talk from the guy whose sleep is more messed up than anybody's," muttered Pitch, who got edgy when she wasn't active. She had a lot more patience for Griffin's plans when climbing was involved.

Ben glared at her resentfully, but could only make out her outline — or was that Savannah? "Yeah, well, these creeps could use a little narcolepsy right now. And no ferret to wake them up."

It would have been too risky to ease the door open and peer into the house, so the team was conducting surveillance purely by listening. Conversation between the two men was sparse, but they were clearly still awake and moving around. There had been no sound from Luthor at all.

"Those awful, low-down, animal-abusing criminals," Savannah seethed. "How strong a tranquilizer did they use on the poor sweetie?"

"What time is it?" Logan yawned.

"About two minutes after the last time you asked," Griffin said quietly. "Essential conversation only. We don't want Swindle to know he's got company."

"An actor thrives on lines," Logan warned.

Pitch had a suggestion. "Why don't you portray a character who's taken a vow of silence?"

"Back off, Melissa," Savannah ordered in a low voice. "You're touching my elbow,"

"No, I'm not," the shy girl replied. "I'm over here behind Logan."

The image of a large hairy tarantula crawling up her arm caused Savannah to draw in a horrified breath. Before it reemerged as a scream, Griffin clamped a hand over her mouth. A short dance ensued.

"Calm down, there's no spider," Ben whispered urgently. "It's just Ferret Face's tail." He pushed the small animal higher under his shirt.

"You know," Melissa commented in her usual quiet manner, "I haven't heard any sound from up there for quite a while."

They listened, tense with excitement.

Swindle's voice, talking to himself, muttered, "Figures. He snores." There followed the grating sounds of someone trying to get comfortable on a couch with creaking springs.

Five minutes passed. Then ten.

So slowly it was practically painful, Griffin inched open the door and peered through the crack. The small house was dim, but the day's storm clouds had broken enough to let in some moonlight. Palomino's pudgy form was scrunched in a threadbare loveseat. His hired man was sprawled in an easy chair. Both were fast asleep, openmouthed and snoring. Between them lay the big Doberman, curled up on a small braided rug, still dead to the world.

"This is it," Griffin whispered. "Logan—get into position."

The young actor retreated to the wooden cellar doors and climbed back to the weeds and mud of the yard. There, he reclaimed the rickety wagon they'd found on the property and pulled it around to the front walk, wincing at the squeak of the rusty wheels. If the plan was successful, the rest of the team would be coming out the door with Luthor in less than a minute.

Inside the house, Griffin, Ben, Savannah, Pitch, and Melissa stepped up to floor level, and crept silently across the parlor. Operation Hideout had reached its most delicate moment. It only remained to grab the dog and spirit him out to the waiting wagon. The trick was to do this just a few feet away from two sleeping enemies.

They arranged themselves around Luthor—two on each flank, and Savannah at the dog's large head. Griffin mouthed the command without uttering a sound: *One, two, three—now!*

The original lift almost scuttled the plan. Luthor was a load, his muscular bulk awkward and unevenly distributed. The first few steps toward the exit were less silent than Griffin had hoped for, but Swindle and his associate slumbered on.

And then fate took a hand. Melissa's phone, which had gotten them so far, issued a low-battery warning in the form of three staccato beeps and a warble.

Palomino and Hiller sat bolt upright and took in the scene with twin gasps of shock and rage. Dragged down by one hundred fifty pounds of tranquilized dog, the team could only watch in dismay as the two men overtook them. Hiller got there first, grabbing the nearest arm.

It was Ben's, and the action drew Ferret Face out of his cocoon. Squeaking with anger, the little creature went on the attack, leaping onto the man's ankle and digging needle-like claws into his already injured leg. With a howl of protest, Hiller snatched up his cane and golfed the little ferret across the room.

Ben saw red. "Ferret Face!" He let go of Luthor and hurled himself onto Hiller, knocking the man flat on his back.

With Ben no longer holding his end up, the others dropped the Doberman. Frantically, Savannah scrambled to pick him up all by herself — an impossible task.

Swindle brushed her away. "He's not your dog — he's mine!"

Wild with fear for her beloved Luthor, Savannah pounded her fists against Palomino's chest. It took Griffin and Pitch to pull her away. Melissa yanked Ben to his feet, and the five backed toward the door.

"I'm not leaving without Luthor!" Savannah shrilled.

"We can't help him now —" Griffin tried to explain, but the girl's crazed struggles made it impossible for him to communicate that their only option was to retreat and regroup.

It took all the team members to get the door open and drag her out.

Logan and his wagon were right there. "Where's Luthor?" he demanded, bewildered.

The cottage door was slammed and locked in their faces.

The chaos rang through the quiet countryside.

"Ferret Face is still in there!" Ben shouted.

"He can look after himself," Griffin promised, hoping it was the truth.

Savannah was wailing now, shaking loose of her

264

friends and barreling headlong back to the door, ready to break it down if need be. *"Luthor! Sweetie!"*

Inside, the atmosphere was not much calmer. Palomino and Hiller were chasing Ferret Face around the small house, and not very successfully. The little creature darted from mantel to bookcase, scooting through their legs and under the furniture. Savannah's screaming and banging on the door echoed in the enclosed space.

"We've got to shut her up before somebody calls the cops!" Hiller panted.

Swindle made an unathletic leap for the furry gray tail. The ferret wriggled out of his grasp, lunged through the air, and landed on Luthor's haunch. There, the small animal performed the task he had been trained for—administering a wake-up nip to a slumbering host.

For the first time in more than fourteen hours, Luthor came to life and took in the unfamiliar surroundings. He was with two men he distinctly remembered disliking. He was pretty sure both of them had been mean to him.

And then his sharpest sense—his hearing—came back to him in a rush. Savannah was out there somewhere, screaming in distress. She needed him, and he wasn't there for her.

He got to his feet with a bark that rattled the rafters. He made several runs for the door, bouncing back in painful frustration. She was still calling his name, still frantically upset. And he knew, with all the loyalty of more than a century of Doberman breeding, that there was no house that could keep him from her.

It was just a matter of effort.

44

The big dog unleashed a barrage on the cottage that was terrible to behold.

Ferret Face hid under the easy chair as Luthor flung his full weight repeatedly against every inch of the walls in search of a weak spot that might allow him to get through to Savannah. His roar was earsplitting. Furniture flew in all directions, curtain rods came crashing down, wood splintered, mirrors shattered.

"Get the dart gun!" Palomino yelped in desperation.

Hiller picked up his cane and thumped for the exit. "No chance, boss! I quit!"

Swindle ducked as Luthor sailed past, knocking over tall shelves, sending books and knickknacks flying in all directions. "Me first!" he yelled. He beat his man to the door, flung it wide, and fled.

His first step outside was into the wagon. His momentum sent it rolling across the property down the gentle slope. He rode like a novice skateboarder, back ramrod straight, chubby arms windmilling in a desperate bid to maintain balance. A gasp of terror was torn from his throat as he jounced into the road just as a pair of headlights loomed out of the darkness on a collision course.

"*Stop!*" he wheezed.

A split second before impact, the vehicle screeched to a halt.

Mr. Bing jumped out and stared at the cause of the near accident. "*You!* Where are our children?"

Not even when he'd been robbed of a million-dollar baseball card had S. Wendell Palomino felt so completely dazed, outsmarted, and outnumbered. More cars were arriving—the rest of the parents, no doubt. He should be saying something to them, giving them a piece of his mind about their terrible, lawless kids. Yet as he climbed unsteadily out of the wagon that had very nearly become his coffin, it was all he could do to point vaguely in the direction of the house.

The new arrivals spilled out of their vehicles and rushed over the wet terrain to the cottage just as Luthor blasted out the door. He joined Savannah in a joyous lovefest on the front walkway, complete with human kisses and very sloppy canine licks. For the dog whisperer, this reunion could not have been sweeter. She was positive that, if Swindle had been allowed to board a plane with the Doberman, she might never have laid eyes on her Luthor again.

Mrs. Drysdale embraced both daughter and dog, choking back a tear. "Aw, honey. I know it feels good now, but it's only going to be twice as painful when you have to give him up."

Savannah unburied her face from Luthor's short black-and-tan fur to beam at her mother. "But we *don't* have to give him up!"

Mr. Drysdale appeared at his wife's side. "Mr. Palomino may not be the nicest person in the world, but he still has the court order on his side."

"Not anymore!" Pitch pulled the document from the Cedarville pound out of her pocket and unfolded it triumphantly in front of the Drysdales. "See? This proves Swindle gave up his dog when he moved out of Cedarville. When you adopted Luthor, it was one-hundred-percent legal. He's *yours*!"

The Drysdales looked in amazement from the paper to Pitch and finally to their daughter and her beloved Doberman.

"Well," Mr. Drysdale said emotionally, "it seems as if this might be the happy ending we were hoping for."

There were nods of agreement from anxious parents reunited at last with their missing campers.

"Not yet!" declared a strident voice.

The Slovaks' car had been at the back of line, so Ben's mother and father were the last to hustle onto the scene.

"Where's my baby?" bellowed Estelle Slovak. "Where's Benjamin?"

Snickers soon morphed into concern as the company looked around.

"Wait a minute," Griffin blurted, confused. "Where *is* Ben?"

At that moment, a small furry form burst out of the cottage, stopped on a dime on the front step, and paused, sniffing the air. It took Ferret Face barely an instant to locate his master, sprawled on the wet ground, fast asleep from the stresses of the night. He hopped onto Ben's stomach, burrowed beneath his T-shirt, and delivered a small bite.

"Ow!" Ben sat up, rubbing his eyes, and was surprised to find himself the center of attention. "What did I miss?"

His mother scooped him into a hug that bordered on a wrestling move. "I could kill you," she said adoringly.

"Uh, excuse me, folks," Dominic Hiller called in an embarrassed tone. "Could any of you give us a ride to the nearest town? We've had a little — car trouble."

Mrs. Drysdale's eyes widened in outage. "You must be joking! You two bullies threatened our children and put them in danger! And *that man*" — pointing at Palomino — "tried to cheat us out of our pet!"

"More than a pet!" Savannah chimed in. "A member of the family!"

"And you helped!" Logan accused Hiller, mustering all his acting skill to portray a lawyer delivering a devastating denunciation in court. "You tried to dognap Luthor at the Showdown!"

"You took out a court order against us," Mr. Drysdale added. He took the dog-pound form from Pitch and waved it angrily. "And you deliberately hid this evidence so the judge would rule against us! How do you explain that?"

Short, pudgy Palomino drew himself up to his full height, which was still a head shorter than Hiller. "I forgot."

Griffin could hardly believe his ears. "You *forgot*?"

"I forgot I gave the dog up," Swindle said stubbornly. "I thought he was still mine. It was an honest mistake."

"Honest!" Savannah spat, squeezing Luthor tighter. "You shouldn't be allowed to use that word, Mr. Palomino! Too bad there's no court order for that."

"Maybe not," said her father, glaring at Palomino. "But if you come near my family or any of these kids again, we're going to take this evidence to Judge Bittner and have you arrested for fraud. Now start walking. No one's going to drive you anywhere."

Luthor underscored this statement with a threatening growl — a reminder that the vicious guard dog he had once been could still be called to active duty if necessary.

"Come on, boss," Hiller put in quickly. "It's a nice night for a stroll."

It was just about the opposite of that. The warm muggy air buzzed with mosquitoes, and the pitch-black rural night made it impossible to navigate a dirt road that had been turned into a muddy minefield of puddles. Yet the cottage was no longer an alternative — not with the inside trashed, and the animal that had trashed it wide awake and stationed between them and the front door.

Swindle and his hired man sloshed off into the darkness, utterly defeated. Twice S. Wendell Palomino had gone up against The Man With The Plan. And twice he'd been sent packing.

Mr. Drysdale let out a long breath and addressed his daughter. "Say good-bye to Luthor, honey. We'll take him home, and you'll see him at the end of the summer." He regarded the other parents. "We should get these six back to their camps."

Ben looked up in dismay. "Back to Camp Endless? Aw!"

"You'll have a good time," his mother said firmly. It was an order.

"You wouldn't want to miss the next zombie apocalypse," his father added.

Logan seemed pleased to be returning to Ta-da! "Mary Catherine still has to feed me grapes."

"And, Griffin—no more plans," Mrs. Bing stated pointedly.

"I promise," her son replied. "I think the delivery truck guys are onto us, anyway."

Mr. Bing took out his car keys. "We can call the camps along the way. You've all got a lot of explaining to do."

"*And* a lot of apologizing," added Mr. Dukakis, although he was secretly proud. He'd always known that camp would help his shy daughter come out of her shell.

As the parents headed for the cars, the six team members hung back. They would surely be resuming their summers in deep trouble with their respective camps. This was their one chance to savor the moment of victory.

"I'm not sorry for anything," Savannah told Griffin in a low voice.

"It was totally worth it." Melissa's furtive eyes emerged from behind her hair to meet five other pairs in complete and total agreement.

"It might be even more worth it than we know," Pitch told them. "I saw a paper in Swindle's SUV that was kind of like Luthor's family history. It said he's descended from some kind of Doberman royalty. He's probably worth a fortune."

"Considering the amount of dog food he inhales, you should just about break even," Ben commented.

Savannah could not have been less interested. "It doesn't matter, because he's not for sale. You can't put a value on Luthor. He's priceless."

EPILOGUE:
WHAT I DID FOR MY SUMMER VACATION

Savannah Drysdale:
I lost the love of my life and got him back again. (PS, he's a dog.)

Ben Slovak:
I was away at camp, but I slept through most of the important parts.

Melissa Dukakis:
I won performer of the year and went into retirement, all on the same day.

Antonia Benson:
Nothing exciting ever happens to me. I was bored out of my mind.

Logan Kellerman:
I discovered how many hamburgers Abraham Lincoln could fit under his hat. (Six.)

Griffin Bing:
I proved once again that nothing is impossible if you have the right plan.

About the Author

Gordon Korman's first four books featuring Griffin Bing and his friends were *Swindle, Zoobreak, Framed,* and *Showoff.* His other books include *This Can't be Happening at Macdonald Hall* (published when he was fourteen); *The Toilet Paper Tigers*; *Radio Fifth Grade*; the trilogies Island, Everest, Dive, Kidnapped, and Titanic; and the series On the Run. He lives in New York with his family and can be found on the Web at www.gordonkorman.com.